To my friend
Bill Forst

Together at the
University of
Heidelberg
1965-66

# THE
# PERFECT WAR

Sam L. Pfiester

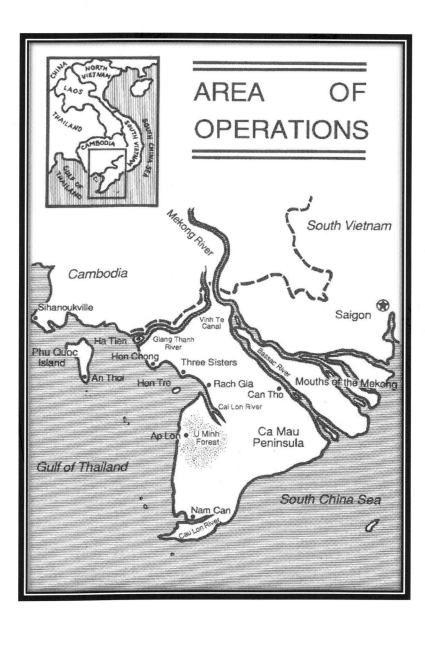

AREA OF OPERATIONS

For he today that sheds his blood with me
Shall be my brother; be he ne'er so vile,
This day shall gentle his condition.

*Henry V,* Act IV, Scene iii

Dedicated to River Ratus Americanus
a band of brothers.

APRIL 1971
SAIGON

The young naval lieutenant gazed across the simmering, grease-stained tarmac of Ton Son Nhut's runways. He, along with the other passengers on Embassy Flight 561, had been waiting impatiently in the sterile out-processing facility since early morning. Soon they would be leaving Saigon for Bangkok, New Delhi, Karachi, Riyadh, Torrejon, and Paris. Today was DEROS, his last day in Vietnam.

He looked down at his khaki uniform, wrinkled and unkempt from months of storage in a duffle bag. The stiff crown of his hat squeezed his forehead. For the past year he had worn loose-fitting black pajamas, standard dress for the native Vietnamese of the southern delta. Now his naval uniform felt uncomfortably constricting.

His thoughts skipped insequentially. Faces of people flashed through his mind — the Dai Uy, Holloman, Sanchez, Thanh — people whose influence had changed his life but whom he would never see again. Never again...the words echoed in his thoughts. Never again would he sail the Gulf of Thailand or patrol the rivers and canals of Kien Giang Province. Never again would he spend mosquito-plagued nights atop the cabin of a fifty-foot junk trying to ambush an elusive enemy. Never again, except on the backroads of his memory. He smiled to himself. A phrase crossed his mind that his grandmother had often repeated: *the best part of the remembering is the rearranging.*

A youthful, trim-cut army sergeant interrupted his thoughts. "Excuse me, Lieutenant. Your Freedom Bird is loading."

The young soldier's cocky self-assurance and starched fatigues reminded him of his own appearance when he had first arrived in Vietnam a year ago.

"How long have you been in-country?"

"One-hundred-and-twelve days and counting, sir. And the day I DEROS they'll hear me holler all the way to Macon, Georgia."

"Here. Go buy yourself a drink." He handed the young sergeant a thick roll of Vietnamese piasters, worth several hundred dollars even at the official exchange rate. Experiencing a strange sense of loss, Alexander stepped into the waiting airplane.

# PART ONE

# HA TIEN

# Chapter I

APRIL 1970
HA TIEN

Lt. J.D. Alexander looked out the window of the canary yellow passenger jet as it began its descent to Ton Son Nhut airport. He was surprised at the peaceful and pastoral appearance of the Vietnamese countryside. He had expected a landscape cratered by bombing.

"It doesn't look like war to me." The comment came from a pimple-faced soldier sitting next to Alexander.

"Not from this altitude, anyway."

"Thank god we're finally here. My ass feels like I've been riding sidesaddle. Twenty-eight hours from San Fran on this frigging airplane!"

Alexander concurred and casually queried, "Do you know where you'll be stationed?"

"At MACV headquarters in Saigon. My brother says it's safer there than Chicago. He was in Nam two years ago."

The response bothered Alexander. That kind of attitude was one of the reasons this war kept dragging on. Eighteen weeks of counterinsurgency training had reinforced his belief in America's involvement in Vietnam. He firmly believed in the moral imperative to contain communism before it spread to the rest of Southeast Asia. He considered troops who vied for desk jobs as not much better than the student protestors — a bunch of kids afraid of their own insignificance.

"How old are you?" Alexander asked.

"Nineteen, and with any luck I'll be home for number twenty. Three-hundred-and-sixty-four days to go!"

"There's a way to get home even faster, you know," said Alexander.

"How, sir?" The question seemed to baffle the young soldier.

"By simply finishing the job. If the military could get the politicians and protestors out of our hair, we could end this mess in less than a year. Unlike in politics, in war there can be no substitute for victory." Alexander was about to say more, but the wheels of the jet touched the runway. Forgetting his indignation, he pushed his cap low over his forehead and took a deep breath.


Three days later, after in-processing through a confusion of standing lines and red-tape, Alexander's sense of purpose was no less clearly defined. He was, however, anxious to leave Saigon. The capital city was crowded and filthy. Congested traffic clogged the streets and filled the air with thick exhaust fumes. Mobs of strange-looking people blocked the sidewalks. Street vendors hawked American goods on the black market. At street corners dirty children begged for souvenirs. Saigon was home to two million refugees, most of them living in filth and squalor. Saigon might be safer than Chicago, but after three days Alexander was eager to get to his new duty station, a place called Ha Tien, somewhere on the Cambodian border.

Finding passage to IV Corp naval headquarters at An Thoi on Phu Quoc island had been a hassle. Eventually Alexander secured a seat on a Vietnamese Air Cofat C-47 cargo flight. He and his gear had barely disembarked on the island before the airplane pivoted on its tail wheels to take off, blowing dust and gravel from the props in his face. A diminutive Vietnamese man, about to slam the airplane's door, grinned and flashed Alexander the two-fingered salute for victory, in Vietnam the symbol for peace. Probably some damn Vietcong, Alexander thought, but he waved back anyway.

The runway was more than a mile from the U.S. Navy base at the tip of the island. Alexander looked at his newly-issued gear that lay heaped around his feet. He couldn't leave it on the runway, but lugging it to the base was impractical. He smelled the fresh sea breeze and glanced at the surrounding hills, once again surprised by the natural beauty of the countryside.

In the distance he saw a trail of dust headed in his direction. Soon he could make out a jeep barreling toward the runway. When the jeep skidded to a halt beside his pile of gear, he jumped aside to avoid being run over.

From under an Australian bush hat a familiar face smiled up at him. Alexander recognized David Holloman, his shipmate for two years when they were stationed aboard a gasoline tanker that hauled avgas and diesel from Danang to the DMZ.

"Well, kiss a Chinese duck!" exclaimed Holloman. "If it's not Lieutenant J.D. Alexander. I thought it might be you...heard yesterday you'd been assigned to IV Corp. Welcome to scenic South Vietnam, Alex."

"Holloman!" Alexander exclaimed, grabbing his old friend's outstretched hand. "You're a sight for sore eyes. What are you doing here? I thought you were assigned to the Delta."

Holloman looked like a postcard warrior: tall and handsome, fitted out in starched, tiger-striped jungle fatigues, polished combat boots, and with a .38 caliber Smith and Wesson strapped to his side.

"Fate has thrown us together again, my short Texas buddy. When I was processing through Saigon last week, they changed my assignment to senior advisor Coastal Group 44. They told me you got Coastal Group 43. Look out ladies, here we come!"

"I can't believe it, Holloman. So where is 44 located? I'll be operating out of a place called Ha Tien."

"Same here, buddy. I was there this morning. It's an absolute, third world armpit on the Cambodian border, two hours by boat across the Gulf. Our living quarters are a tad, well, rustic. It makes An Thoi look like Pearl Harbor. Come on, throw your gear in the back, and let's get you checked in."

"Together again," said Alexander as the jeep headed for the base. Holloman's driving had not improved since Alexander's last ride with him. "Somehow it's fitting. Remember how we craved an in-country assignment when we were anchored off Cua Viet, watching the marines take all the shit. Well, here we are. This is where the action is, and I'm loving it."

"What are you talking about — loving it? I requested shore duty, remember, but in southern California," said Holloman. "Take a look at that beautiful piece of suburbia," he continued, pointing toward a group of dwellings next to the dirt road.

Alexander stared at the ramshackle rows of shanties made from cardboard and smashed beer cans. Vietnamese children, naked from the waist down, waved as the jeep drove rapidly through the squalid barrio.

"This is home to the Vietnamese who work on the base. These gooks, Sancho, are who you'll be risking your life for," quipped Holloman. "I'm for keeping the Vietcong out of Honolulu, but risk my ass for this...?"

The naval base was surrounded by a high chain-link fence and triple rows of concertina wire. Two American marines smartly saluted as the jeep proceeded through the gate. The contrast between the filthy village and the orderly naval base was startling. Inside the base neat rows of quonset huts lined the entry drive. A group of shirtless American soldiers were playing volleyball in a sandy field beyond a parade ground where a freshly-painted flagpole proudly displayed the Stars and Stripes. In the harbor Alexander could see docks and several small riverine craft. Everywhere he looked the naval base was two-blocked and orderly.

Holloman stopped the jeep in front of a quonset hut and directed Alexander toward a door bearing a sign that was intended to read 'In Processing.' Someone had changed the word 'In' to read 'Mind.'

"That's check-in," explained Holloman. "After you finish with the paperwork, meet me at the O-Club over by the docks. We'll take a Swift boat to Ha Tien in a couple of hours, so we have time for an early afternoon cocktail or two. Glad you're here you, Alex. Glad we're in this together, buddy."

Alexander left his gear in the jeep and walked inside the quonset hut, which looked like any other shipboard administrative office. The air conditioning felt cool on his face. Since his orders had been changed recently there was some confusion, but within an hour he had his pay status, mailing address, and other records properly established. He met briefly with the commanding officer, Commander Schoen, who welcomed him aboard and outlined several standing regulations, premier of which was to observe Cambodian neutrality.

Except for the sandbags that lined the outside walls of the quonset huts, nothing about the base conveyed the appearance of a war zone. Alexander was surprised, however, when he stepped inside the officers' club. Its interior was as plush as any O-club in the States. The soft couches, game tables, and rows of slot machines made him wonder if such comforts might be a distraction from the real objectives.

A large screened porch along the back of the club overlooked the deep, blue water of the bay.

"Alexander, over here."

Holloman was sitting on the porch. Already four empty glasses were on his table. He never let the bartender remove empties until he was ready to leave.

"Up to your old tricks, I see," said Alexander, slightly irritated. "We're in a combat zone, Holloman. Maybe you should go a little easy on the booze."

"Good lord, Alex! Can't I have three drinks before you accuse me of dereliction of duty? Sit down and relax. Have a gin and tonic. It prevents malaria, you know." Holloman held up his hand for two more drinks.

Alexander hesitated, but joined his friend, who again assured him they had nothing else to do but wait for the Swift boat to take them to Ha Tien.

It seemed only natural for the two to be back together. For nearly two years they had been the only unmarried officers aboard a small gasoline tanker that hauled diesel and avgas from large commercial tankers anchored in Danang Harbor north to Cua Viet near the DMZ. After spending days and months at sea, Alexander's and Holloman's escapades in port became legend. Once in Guam after crossing the Pacific from Pearl Harbor, both had been thrown in the brig over a fight with a bar owner whose pinball machine had swallowed their coin. In Singapore for ship repairs, after standing underway watch for more than one hundred days, they had flipped a coin for a whore. As a result, Holloman contracted gonorrhea and Alexander nearly missed ship's muster because of a dalliance with a British nurse.

While hauling fuel for months along the Vietnamese coast in I Corp, they had observed incoming artillery on the marine's bases, but had never participated in the fighting. When their Westpac tour was up, Alexander requested an in-country assignment back to Vietnam. Holloman derided his judgment and asked for shore duty at a weather station near Big Sur, California. Holloman doubled over with laughter when Alexander received a postcard ordering him to report for naval advisory duty in Vietnam. The next day Holloman received similar orders.

"Come on, Alex, grab your gear," said Holloman finally, emptying his last drink. "The Swift driver has started the engines. By the time we get to Ha Tien, the sun will be under the yardarm."

The shadows were lengthening across the bay. Coconut palms near the beach waved gracefully as Holloman helped carry Alexander's gear to the dock and threw it on the boat's prow. When Alexander stepped aboard he immediately felt the powerful vibration of the engines. The fifty-foot, aluminum-hulled Swift boat, originally designed to service offshore oil platforms in the Gulf of Mexico, carried twin .50 caliber machine guns mounted fore and aft.

After passing the sheltered bay and turning toward the mainland, the full force of the wind caught the prow, causing the boat to roll as it sliced through the waves at better than twenty-five knots. Alexander inhaled deeply. The fresh sea breeze was exhilarating. Finally, the months of tedious schooling and dislocated days were at an end.

# Chapter II

Two hours later, in the fading sunlight, Alexander caught his first glimpse of Ha Tien. An arm of land cradled a broad, shallow harbor at the mouth of the Giang Thanh River. A village of thatched houses and several two-story plaster buildings huddled along the spit of land. Small, unpainted fishing vessels were tied to narrow docks that stretched from the muddy shore. An old French plantation house with a steep-pitched tin roof and wide verandas stood vigil on a low promontory overlooking the bay.

"That's home," Holloman yelled over the roar of the boat's engines. "Ha Tien. Home sweet home. The advisors for both our coastal groups are headquartered in the compound on the hill. We offer no running water, no flushing toilets, and no room service. Except for those minor details it's everything your navy recruiter promised."

Alexander looked up the bluff at the stately old manor and wondered about the French colonists who had lived there fifty years ago. In the last rays of sunlight the house seemed to blush like a coral-colored mirage.

The Swift boat dropped the two advisors next to the steep path leading up to the back veranda. Both men were out of breath when they reached the house. On closer scrutiny, Alexander saw that the house was dirty and dilapidated.

"I sleep on the porch overlooking the bay," Holloman said, after showing Alexander where to throw his gear. "From here we occasionally catch a slight breeze. Be sure to put mosquito netting over your cot."

"Where are the other advisors?" asked Alexander. "And when do we get briefed by our predecessors?"

"I forgot to tell you. Our predecessors, as you call them, shipped out a week ago. The two enlisted advisors are probably downtown drinking a beer at Ong Minh's. They'll be home for chop-chop. By the way, we're under a red alert tonight. The VC are supposed to mortar Ha Tien, at least that's what the intelligence boys told me this morning. I think they create red alerts to fight boredom. This place hasn't been hit since Tet two years ago."

"Do you mean the Navy assigned us as senior advisors to a Vietnamese coastal patrol group without any overlap from our predecessors? What a breakdown in procedure!" Alexander was incredulous.

"I have a feeling, Alex, that your duty-honor-country perfectionism is a tad out of place. You'd better set your sights a little lower. This ain't Pearl Harbor."

"All I expect is ordinary competence. For the two of us to be senior advisors with no overlap from our predecessors and no onsite training is absolutely asinine."

Holloman removed his holster and boots and lay back on his cot. "That's the way it goes in the hinterlands. In the morning I'll introduce you to your Vietnamese counterpart. He's your type of guy, full of vinegar. I've never seen him when he wasn't grinning."

"What's his name?" asked Alexander, still dismayed at the news that he and Holloman were in charge of the advisory efforts with no real knowledge of what to expect. He efficiently began rigging the mosquito netting over a cot.

"Khuay," responded Holloman. "Dai Uy Khuay, but we just call him Dai Uy. Reminds me of a Mexican jumping bean. The man has more energy than any other two gooks put together, even in this heat."

"Good," replied Alexander, who had been warned about the lackadaisical leadership of the Vietnamese armed forces. The instructor he had most admired at counterinsurgency school had told him that if South Vietnam lost the war, corrupt and inept leadership would be the fundamental cause. "And my other 43 advisor...the one you say is drinking down in the village, what's his story?"

"That would be Sanchez," Holloman answered. "Hispanic, boatswains mate first class, appears to be a top-notch man, except that he's a little queer on the gooks. This is his third in-country tour. Two years ago he was shot up on a river patrol in the Bassac, and he still re-upped. Dog ass me why."

Alexander liked what he heard about his counterpart, and it at least sounded like his assistant advisor knew the ropes. Perhaps the raw material was present to shape the coastal group into a first-class fighting unit. "And what about your counterpart and assistant advisor?"

"Mine," said Holloman, "are not exactly corp material. My counterpart, a lieutenant junior grade, has a chip on his shoulder and a bad overbite. And my NCO, Westy, is a short-timer. Only three weeks until his DEROS, so, he, as you would put it, lacks motivation."

Alexander tied the last loop on the mosquito netting and began organizing his mound of gear into neat stacks. Darkness had fallen. He could hear unfamiliar sounds of night outside their compound. "Tell me what you know about the river operations. What's their scope?"

"Fairly straight forward, as far as I can tell. For the past ten months our junks have joined the American forces in patrolling the Giang Thanh River and Vinh Te Canal, which define the Vietnam/Cambodian border from the coast to the Mekong. The object is to stop any VC traffic from crossing into Vietnam. For the most part it's fighting mosquitoes and..."

An ear-splitting blast shook the ground. Startled, the two Americans stared at each other for a brief instant. Another round landed just down the hill from the advisor's compound.

"I'll be goddamn...mortars! Hit the bunker!" Holloman grabbed his helmet and rushed out the back. Seizing his flak jacket and M-16, Alexander hurriedly followed. Dropping to his hands and knees, he crawled behind Holloman through the sandbagged opening. Inside, the bunker was dark, muddy, and smelled of urine.

"Goddamn it," Holloman groaned. "Can you believe the fucking mud. If the mortars don't..." *Crumpf.* Another earthshaking explosion split the air.

"What the shit is going on?" demanded Alexander, expecting at any moment a squad of VC to overrun the compound. Three more mortar rounds landed in quick succession farther down the hill. "Where's your rifle?"

"I left it in the house," groaned Holloman.

Alexander started to make a comment, but kept silent. He had a splitting headache and his mouth felt like dry ice. The stench in the bunker nearly made him sick at his stomach, but he was at least prepared for an attack. For a long while he and Holloman listened intently for the sound of approaching footsteps, expecting their compound to be overrun. But after the last series of explosions, an eerie silence prevailed.

"Holy shit, Alex, how in the hell did we end up

*here*, in a third-world dump risking our ass for what? Hey, where you going?"

Alexander was leaving the bunker. "To get a drink of water. Looks like the party is over."

Alexander made his way back to the house. The interior was pitch dark and unfamiliar. Feeling his way to the kitchen, he reached the refrigerator, opened it and felt for a bottle of water. Grabbing the first bottle he found, he raised it to his mouth, took a big gulp, and immediately spewed out the foul tasting liquid. Gagging, he stumbled to the back porch. Holloman had emerged from the bunker and was shaking the mud from his socks. "What in the world have you done? Smells like you found the *nuoc mam*."

"What *is* this shit?"

"The gooks use it for spice," chuckled Holloman. "I've never seen any of them drink it straight, though. What about the mortar attack? Can you believe it?"

"It feels like someone hit me in the mouth with a dead squirrel," sputtered Alexander and moved to the back veranda for some fresh air.

When he finally recovered and returned to the house, a small kerosene lantern had been lit. Two enlisted men stood next to Holloman. They were discussing the mortar attack. All three looked up when he walked into the light.

"Men," said Holloman, "meet our new advisor, Lieutenant Alexander. Alex, this is Westy," Holloman said, introducing a short, pink-cheeked sailor.

25

Westy mumbled something under his breath about new meat for the mosquitoes and gave a nonchalant nod. Alexander, still coughing from the *nuoc mam*, acknowledged the introduction.

"And this is Sanchez, your other 43 advisor."

At the light's fringe stood a tall, slender Hispanic wearing loose fitting black pajamas like the local Vietnamese fishermen. His eyes were dark as porphyry. When he extended an outstretched hand, a quixotic smile spread below his wispy mustache. Alexander noted the ceremony of saluting officers had not reached Ha Tien.

Westy was explaining that he and Sanchez had been drinking beer in the village when the mortars hit. "We just ducked under the table and stayed there until it stopped," he said.

"Why would they mortar us now?" asked Holloman. "It's been quiet in Ha Tien for months. Has anything happened upriver to provoke a mortar attack?"

"Not really," Sanchez responded. "A hamlet was mortared a couple of weeks ago. Maybe the Dai Uy will know something."

"What do we do now?" interjected Alexander. "How do we retaliate?"

Westy laughed out loud. "Retaliate?" he repeated. "Hey, man, this is the Nam. Ninety percent of the time you don't know who's shooting at you or where they're shooting from. Charlie's long gone by now, probably in bed with his old lady right here in Ha Tien. Retaliate? You must have been reading books."

Alexander's face showed his surprise. Not to respond to a direct attack by the enemy was contrary to everything he had been taught. Yet he wasn't confident enough to demand a response and in fact, could not think of how to direct one. After listening for nearly an hour to the other advisors speculate on the cause of the mortar attack, Alexander excused himself and retired to his cot, physically exhausted. He lay there half numb but unable to sleep the rest of the night. At the first faint light of early morning, he quietly dressed and walked outside to watch the sun rise over the bay. He was observing the early dawn activity among the fishing boats when Holloman walked up beside him.

"Good morning, Alex. How did you sleep?"

"I didn't."

"I have a feeling for the next year a night's sleep will be a luxury," continued Holloman. "Shit, what about last night? Who *are* these bastards?"

"Don't ask me," Alexander responded. Lack of sleep made him brusque. "When can I meet my counterpart?"

"After breakfast I'll give you a tour of the village and then we'll meet the Dai Uy."

"Where's Sanchez?"

"He and Westy live in the village with a couple of local girls. You and I might look into a similar arrangement. They're some good-looking ladies in this one-horse hole."

Alexander's was dismayed. "Is it safe in the village? Anybody with a hand grenade could kill them."

"They think it's safer than here and after last night, who are we to argue?"

After a quick breakfast of C-Rats, Alexander and Holloman walked down to the village. Alexander observed that the Vietnamese peasants dressed uniformly in black pajamas and conical straw hats, and bustled along the dirt road carrying heavy loads balanced on shoulder poles, or squatted on their haunches selling goods and conversing loudly with each other. Their conversation reminded Alexander of geese. Most of the older women chewed betel nut, which stained their gums and teeth a dull-red carmine color. Thatched houses lined the dirty, shallow bay. Long, narrow wooden docks extended from the thatched houses to open latrines built over the bay. Next to several houses piles of shrimp and stingray drying in the sun lay heaped on straw mats. The decaying smell of seafood mixed with dust and brine broadcast a terrific odor.

The dirt road widened into a communal square lined by several two-story plaster buildings which formed a central square. Every structure in the village, including the docks and small fishing boats, looked worn out and in disrepair.

A group of children began following the two Americans. The braver ones smiled and shouted, "Number One, Number One, Amer-i-can," and held out their hands for coins. Alexander reached into his pocket and handed them what change he had.

"Get out of here!" yelled Holloman. The children scattered like wild animals.

"The little peckerheads probably run guns at night for the VC," said Holloman. "In this war, it's hard to tell the cowboys from the Indians."

Holloman stopped in front of a tall palm tree that stood at the side of the road. "This," he explained to Alexander, "is Ha Tien's one claim to fame. According to Ripley's, it's the only palm tree in the world with three heads."

"A three-headed palm tree, Jesus H. Christ." Alexander gave one glance at the tree and impatiently proceeded down the road. As they reached the far side of the village next to the Vietnamese naval base, Holloman pointed up to a granite peak rising a few hundred feet above the coastal plain.

"That's Nui Dai Dung," he said. "It's inside Cambodia and off limits to us, but home to Charlie."

Alexander stared up at the tall hill. He was surprised at its closeness. How could it be a sanctuary for the VC and be so near to the naval base? He recalled the principal order from Commander Schoen was, above all else, to observe Cambodian neutrality.

Holloman's tone became cynical. "We know where the VC resupply originates — twenty miles up the coast at Sihanoukville. We know they have huge supply depots and training centers all along the Cambodian border. But we can't do a frigging thing about it because we observe Cambodia's so-called neutrality."

"Whoever made that rule wasn't standing here when he made it, now was he?" Alexander observed.

The two Americans entered the naval compound. A lackadaisical guard nodded at the gate. Rusty coils of concertina bordered the Vietnamese base on two sides. Only a low rock wall topped with loose strands of barbed wire separated the base from the village. Crates and equipment cluttered the yard. A U.S. Army jeep rested against a dilapidated tin building. The yellow-and-red striped South Vietnamese flag dangled on a weathered, unpainted wooden flagpole. On the bay two newly-built docks berthed an assortment of gunboats.

"This is it," said Holloman, with a sweep of his arm. "Headquarters for the Republic of Vietnam's junk forces in IV Corp, Coastal Groups 43 and 44. What do you think?"

Alexander was silent for a moment. "You're right about one thing. It ain't Pearl Harbor," he admitted.

"I thought you'd be impressed. Not exactly two-blocked and ship-shape, is it? Coastal Group 44's boats are tied up there." Holloman pointed toward the closest dock. "We have all fairly new Yabuta class junks — those painted haze grey with the stand-up cabin. Your boats are tied up at the other dock. You have only four Yabuta class boats. The two low-riding wide junks painted dark green are Xuyen class junks, good for coastal ops but neither can turn around in the river without backing up several times. The junk that looks like an old pirate ship is the Kieng Giang class."

Alexander stared at the assortment of vessels. Each boat was armed with a fifty-caliber machine gun mounted on the foredeck and a thirty caliber mounted aft. Some had mortar racks amidships. None were more than fifty feet long. They all looked terribly cumbersome for river operations. A set of colorful eyes were painted on the nose of each junk.

"The eyes of the dragon," Holloman explained. "The gooks think they keep evil spirits away. No mention of AK-47 rounds."

"What kind of working condition are the junks in?"

"Each coastal group is supposed to keep at least five boats operating at any one time. Scavenging might become our primary duty. So far, the only advice my Vietnamese counterpart has asked for is how to get spare parts."

Holloman led Alexander to the only new Quonset building. They walked down a hall and into a small office where a diminutive Vietnamese officer was pacing the floor and speaking rapidly into a handheld radio. He reminded Alexander of a cricket. Without putting down the radio, the Dai Uy motioned the Americans to take a seat at a small conference table. The chairs were so tiny that Alexander's chin nearly rested on his knees.

The Dai Uy concluded his radio conversation, grinned, and shook Holloman's hand.

"Dai Uy Khuay," said Holloman, "meet your new counterpart, Lieutenant Alexander."

Alexander shook the small hand that seemed as

frail as a child's.

"Very happy you come to Ha Tien," said the Dai Uy with enthusiasm.

Thank god he speaks English, thought Alexander, aware that his limited knowledge of Vietnamese could be dangerous in an emergency.

"Lieutenant Holl-o-man tell me you...he are friends," continued the Dai Uy. "Good. Number one."

"Yes, we served on the same ship," Alexander enunciated slowly.

"Number one. You my counterpart. Now Coastal Group 43 patrol river. Big boss say stop VC from Kambot. OK, we stop," the Dai Uy said as he stepped toward a large topographic map on the wall.

Holloman continued the explanation. "Charlie uses this part of the river to re-supply his Main Force battalions south of here in the U Minh forest. Our job is to form an inland barrier to intercept any supplies he tries to cross along the lower thirty miles of the border. We patrol the river during the day, and at night we set up ambush along the river and the Vinh Te canal."

Alexander stood up, walked to the map, and examined the river. Its lower portion meandered through what showed as mangrove swamps. "How long have we been patrolling the river?" he asked.

"The U.S. has been patrolling it with Swift boats and PBR's for nearly two years. Last year the army put in what they call 'duffle bags', electronic snooping gear, along the Vietnamese side of the river, which alert the artillery to any unauthorized crossing. Our junks moved in several months ago as part of Nixon's Vietnamization program. They aren't as maneuverable as the U.S. riverine boats, but if we spread up and down the river, we can cover a fairly large area with limited firepower. Each junk carries eight to ten Vietnamese sailors," continued Holloman. "Our standing orders are if anything looks suspicious, we shoot first and ask questions later. Nothing complicated about that."

The Dai Uy nodded in approval, apparently pleased with Holloman's explanation, and grinned at Alexander. "Tonight, you go with me on patrol," he said with enthusiasm. "I take you up river. Number one chop-chop. You come here at eighteen hundred. You will like."

Alexander recognized their dismissal. He stood and again shook the Dai Uy's frail hand, but was impressed with the little man's forthrightness and energy.

Returning to the advisor's house, Alexander reviewed in his mind his brief meeting with the Dai Uy. So, tonight was his first patrol. Finally, this was what the months of training and instruction had been for. At least he wouldn't be lying around waiting for a mortar round to fall through the roof.

Late in the afternoon Sanchez walked to the advisor's compound and helped Alexander gather the gear for the patrol. They threw on flak jackets and backpacks, and carried their rifles, radio, and a Starlight scope in an aluminum suitcase to the docks.

Sanchez climbed aboard one of the junks, extended a hand to help Alexander step over the gunwale, then threw his gear on top of the junk's cabin. Alexander followed suit. The Dai Uy was inside the cabin loudly talking into the radio and gave the thumbs up sign when he saw the two Americans.

In a cacophony of shouts and exhaust fumes, the Coastal Group 43 junks started their engines and began backing into the harbor. Sanchez climbed up onto the roof of the command junk's cabin, turned on the portable PRC-25 radio, and checked in with the Naval Operations Center, located aboard a U. S. naval ship — the USS Garret County — anchored two miles offshore. The Dai Uy continued shouting orders over his radio. Alexander joined Sanchez on the cabin roof to remove himself from the pandemonium on deck.

The six junks proceeded slowly across the estuary to a shallow sand bar that separated the bay from the river. When they entered the wide mouth of the river the sailors donned their flak jackets and helmets. More by constraint than design, the junks lined up in single file, the Dai Uy's boat in the lead, and began advancing up river.

At the river's mouth the shoreline was a flat swamp, thickly overgrown with nipa palms and mangrove trees. The first few miles were uninhabited by anything but mosquitoes. A few narrow canals angled from both river banks toward unseen fields beyond the swamp. In the far distance, rising above the line of dense foliage, blue shaded mountains could be seen in Cambodia. Overhead, large thunderheads built lofty designs, accenting the green flatness of land. The river water was a soft, dun color, the consistency of soup.

Sitting on top of the lead boat's cabin of the first boat, Alexander felt terribly exposed and conspicuous. The river banks were no more than fifty yards apart, an easy distance for a sniper, and becoming narrower.

"Ever been shot at along here?" he asked Sanchez calmly, concealing his nervousness.

"A hairpin curve is up ahead in about two more miles," replied Sanchez. He pointed to the map and showed Alexander how to track their position. "Sometimes our second or third boat will take a few sniper shots in the curve. It's an old VC trick. If all our boats return fire, we'd be shooting at ourselves across both sides of the bend."

When the junks approached the curve, the Dai Uy shouted at a sailor, who unexpectedly opened up with the .50 caliber on the Cambodian bank. Alexander was startled at the thunderous sound of the machine gun's deep burping. On the adjacent bank, trees splintered like matchsticks. The Dai Uy looked out the cabin at Alexander and grinned. Alexander smiled back, but thought to himself, if you intended to scare the shit out of me, my little friend, you succeeded.

"The Dai Uy likes to shoot 'em up," Sanchez commented dryly.

Two American PBR's appeared from down river

and whipped past the slow-moving junks. Alexander watched enviously as the American boats roared out of sight.

"PBR's can churn out 38 knots and draw less than twelve inches of water," said Sanchez.

Alexander noted that they carried a crew of four and were equipped with .50 caliber machine guns and automatic grenade launchers. At full speed, he guessed his junks could barely make five knots. They pitched and rolled awkwardly in the wakes left by the PBR's.

During the trip upriver the junks stopped several narrow, open-hulled boats less than twenty feet long, sampans used by the Vietnamese fishermen. The sailors on the junks haphazardly checked for identification papers. Mostly they were interested in accepting a few fish for their supper and in eyeing the young Vietnamese girls riding in the sampans with their families.

As dusk fell the Dai Uy directed where each of the Vietnamese boats were to tie up at a concealed ambush sight in the dense undergrowth along the Cambodian side of the river. Sanchez showed Alexander how to mark each boat's position on the map. When all the other boats were positioned, the Dai Uy headed his command junk back down the narrow river, first by steering toward shore and alternately backing and driving forward until the junk finally pointed downriver. They passed two of the other boats and stationed themselves in the center of the column. A heavy silence displaced the clamor of the motors.

The Dai Uy and Sanchez double-checked each boat's location on their maps. "Number one," said the Dai Uy when both maps matched. "Alex, what you think?"

"Number one," responded Alexander.

The Dai Uy grinned.

Sanchez removed the KAK charts from his back pack, encoded the boats' positions, and relayed the information over the PRC-25 radio to the Naval Operations Center. "NOC keeps track of all the boats on the river so our artillery or choppers won't hit friendlies," he explained to Alex. "At least they're not supposed to."

"What happens if we're ambushed while moving up or down river?" asked Alexander.

"It's impossible to outrun the trap. When the shit hits the fan, we point straight toward shore with all guns firing. First and foremost, though, you call for the Seawolves, which are two Navy choppers stationed on the ship. They usually can get to us within twenty minutes. Give them your coordinates and when they arrive, direct fire. The radio is your best weapon."

Alexander was surprised with the advice. No one at counterinsurgency school had suggested that his radio was his best weapon.

In the glow of a stunning sunset dramatized by lofty thunderheads, Alexander sat on the cabin's roof, idly reflecting on the natural beauty of the river and the surrounding scene. He observed the Vietnamese sailors sitting on their haunches, smoking, and chatting in low voices. He watched as one of them lifted a heavy cardboard carton from the hold. When the lid was raised, dozens of three-inch long cockroaches scattered from the box. Shocked, Alexander watched the cook nonchalantly proceed to scoop rice from the box, paying no attention to the huge insects. He glanced at Sanchez to express his disbelief, but Sanchez was preoccupied with blowing up an air mattress.

Within minutes the cook had several pots steaming over a small butane burner. The aroma reminded him of *nuoc mam* sauce. When the meal was ready the cook gave a muted grunt. Sanchez asked Alexander if he wanted to eat with the Vietnamese.

"No thanks. Sanchez, did you see all those cockroaches in the rice box?"

"Nah, but they boil the rice anyway." Sanchez jumped down, grabbed a bowl, and joined the Vietnamese for the meal, laid out in communal dishes on the deck. Alexander kept to the roof of the cabin and dug a carton of C-rations from his backpack.

After the meal the sailors lounged on deck, smoking and talking in whispers. The Dai Uy kept to himself in his cabin, while Alexander and Sanchez sat on the cabin's roof. Darkness gradually enveloped them. The air was dank and tepid.

"This is all there is to a night ambush," whispered Sanchez. "We spread our boats along the river so nothing of any size can cross."

"What do we do if a sampan comes down the

river? Do we pull it over or what?"

"We open up."

"Without asking questions?"

"We enforce a curfew from dark to dawn. If anything moves, blow it away. If we receive fire, call for the Seawolves. By the way," continued Sanchez, "we can't call in artillery or helicopters on the Cambodian side of the river."

"*What?* Why not?" Alexander knew they couldn't attack into Cambodia, but not returning fire seemed idiotic.

"Those are the rules. No air or artillery support in Cambodia," repeated Sanchez.

Alexander was incredulous. "What kind of a goddamn rule is that?" Not only was he supposed to fight an enemy he knew nothing about, but now he found he could only fight them if they were on the Vietnamese side of the river.

"We shoot and ask questions later," responded Sanchez indifferently. "Have you ever looked through a Starlight scope?"

Sanchez removed the scope from its aluminum case. "You turn it on here," he said. "For sniper work we mount it on M-16's, but for river ops we only use it for recon. Now take a look through the eyepiece."

Alexander held the instrument to his eye. He was amazed. Even in the darkness of the night he could see as clearly as if it were early dawn, except in tones of light green. Slowly he scanned beyond the embankment. The scope's magnifying power made the distant mountains seem nearby. "Quite a gadget," he mumbled.

"Where we are, it's the edge," responded Sanchez from his air mattress. He placed the scope between them. "If you hear anything in the night, check it out with the Starlight."

"Sanchez, have you ever interrogated a VC?" asked Alexander. His curiosity about their enemy had been growing. Who *were* the Vietcong? Was there any way to differentiate them for all the other Vietnamese?

"The only VC I've seen have been dead. Not much to talk to them about."

With that thought in mind, Alexander lay on his air mattress and drifted into a restless sleep, interrupted throughout the night by leaves stirring or soft scurrying sounds on the adjacent bank, causing him to grab the Starlight and scan the shore, fully expecting to find a regiment of VC approaching their position.

As the light of dawn slowly spread across the sky, Alexander watched the cook again open the rice carton, swash away the cockroaches, and measure rice into a cooking pan. When breakfast was ready, the cook looked up at Alexander and offered for him to join the feast. Alexander hesitated, but accepted. He dropped to the deck beside the Dai Uy, handed his bowl to the cook, who filled it with rice and indicated for Alexander to pick from the dishes spread before them. Cautiously Alexander picked up something brown that looked like a piece of fish, put his bowl to his lip like the other sailors, and raked a small portion into his mouth with the unfamiliar chopsticks. The Dai Uy winked at him. Surprisingly the taste was spicy and flavorful, not at all as he had expected.

"*An com*," said the Dai Uy, repeating in American slang, "Chop-chop. You like?"

Alexander nodded. "Number one." Then in faltering Vietnamese he continued, "*mon nay dam da lam.*"

Several of the sailors laughed, but the Dai Uy looked pleased. "You talk Vietnamese. Good. Very good." He then reached into the communal serving dish and dropped a fish head into Alexander's bowl.

Alexander presumed this to be a gesture of hospitality reserved for honored guests. He smiled and said, "Number one," and put the fish head, eyeballs and all, into his mouth. The sailors broke into laughter, which made Alexander wonder if he had been deceived, but the Dai Uy was obviously pleased.

"You like Vietnamese food. Good. Number one."

As soon as breakfast was finished the Dai Uy gave an order over his radio. Boats up and down the river began coughing to a start. The command junk was untied, backed into the current, and pointed upstream. The clamor of its motor displaced the hushed stillness of the early dawn. Alexander climbed back onto the cabin's roof, and following Sanchez' example, put on his flak jacket and helmet.

41

The morning air was clear and invigorating. Alexander felt keenly alert despite his lack of sleep. They passed the two junks that were upriver. Both were stuck high aground. Sailors onboard were shouting and laughing at their predicament. The Dai Uy angrily yelled at each boat as they drove by.

"They tied up with too short of a line, and the tide dropped," explained Sanchez. "It really pisses off the Dai Uy."

Soon the river was scarcely wider than the length of the junks. Thick foliage along each bank was sometimes broken by stretches of broad, flat grasslands that stretched to the far horizon. Six-foot tall termite mounds punctuated the landscape. After more than an hour's journey, just beyond a broad bend in the river, a tiny hamlet of thatched huts built beside the muddy river bank came into sight. The boats halted alongside a narrow, rickety wooden dock.

The Dai Uy jumped lightly to the boardwalk, followed by Alexander and Sanchez. They climbed up a muddy slope and came to a path between several small thatched huts that led to an outdoor coffee shop. They sat outdoors on small wooden chairs and ordered hot tea from a toothless old woman. Several peasants, mainly old women and small naked children, followed their party and stared at the two Americans. The children reached out their filthy hands for gifts. Sanchez joked with several of the villagers, which surprised Alexander.

"I didn't know you could speak Vietnamese."

"Just picked up a little here and there," responded Sanchez modestly.

The peasants asked shy questions of Sanchez, and when he answered, they giggled. The Dai Uy and Sanchez exchanged a few words in Vietnamese, and then the Vietnamese officer looked at Alexander and abruptly asked, "What you think of night ambush?"

Alexander paused, then spoke with frankness. "I think the VC know where we are."

The Dai Uy was taken aback, but broke into his usual grin. "Maybe so. But he not cross river."

"Not where our boats are," agreed Alexander. Turning to Sanchez, Alexander asked, "What do you think of the ambushes, Sanchez?"

Sanchez shrugged his shoulders. "Our job is to stop the cross-river traffic. We can only stop it where we tie up for ambush."

"But if Charlie knows where we are, it should be easy enough for him to avoid us," reasoned Alexander.

"The junks make so much racket moving up and down river that trying to hide our movement is impossible," responded Sanchez.

"What if we spread the junks farther apart?"

"That's dangerous. A small squad could easily overrun a single junk."

"Alex, I call you Alex," interrupted the Dai Uy. "We can do ambush better. I know how."

"How?"

"In sampans, like fishermen," replied the Dai Uy.

"Fight VC like VC fight. We use sampans."

"Is that not even more dangerous?" asked Alexander, thinking to himself that the old .50 calibers on the junks at least provided a superiority of firepower over AK-47's.

"Yes," grinned the Dai Uy, "but I like to catch Charlie."

Alexander was pleased that the Dai Uy was willing to discuss a change in procedure. His teachers at counterinsurgency school had warned Alexander about their counterparts' resistance to American suggestions. Tact and timing, they had hammered, were the keys to changing procedures. Still, the more Alexander observed the Dai Uy, the less the diminutive Vietnamese officer fit the image of the corrupt, indolent, and risk-averse officers portrayed by the teachers at school.

"Next patrol we do sampan ambush," concluded the Dai Uy. "You like."

Alexander nodded, wondering if the discussion had taken a wrong turn, just as a large, low-riding boat with an extended cabin pulled up to the dock behind the junk. It was packed with Vietnamese peasants. Colorful plastic bags stuffed with produce covered its roof.

"That's the water taxi to Ha Tien," said Sanchez to Alexander. "Time for me to go. We'll switch patrols port and starboard. I'll take the next one. Remember one thing. If the shit hits the fan, call the Seawolves."

Alexander watched Sanchez transfer his gear and

boarded the crowded vessel. He thought to himself that all the fish in the South China sea couldn't get him to crawl into that Vietcong-infested vessel. It didn't seem to bother Sanchez, however. With the last glimpse of the water taxi as it rounded the bend, Alexander felt a loss of confidence. His ties to the Western world were now completely severed.

The remainder of the first patrol was uneventful. Each night the junks set up ambush along a different stretch of the river. Alexander confirmed their position with the Dai Uy and, using the KAK codes, called in the boats' locations to the Navy support ship. During the day the sailors lounged, chatted, ate, and listened to portable radios blaring atonal Vietnamese music. During the night most of them slept below deck except for those on watch duty. Alexander only fitfully dozed, and constantly checked the surrounding shore with the Starlight scope.

Like Sanchez, Alexander made his home on top the roof of the Dai Uy's cabin. He stretched his nylon poncho liner between the radio antenna and the flag shaft to provide shade. From that vantage he caught a slight breeze and, where the foliage was sparse, could see far into Cambodia. The natural tranquility of the surroundings and the placid flow of the muddy river dissipated any thoughts of hostility.

The second afternoon Alexander returned to his aerie and found a Vietnamese sailor lying on his air mattress, enjoying the shade and the view. When the sailor asked him to "souvenir" a C-ration, Alexander angrily ordered the Vietnamese off the air mattress. Later that day as Alexander was relieving himself over the side of the boat, several of the Vietnamese sailors laughed and pointed to his exposed white buttocks. Goddamn gooks, he thought, pulling up his pants.

Twice he tried talking with the Dai Uy, however, the language barrier was too great to carry on any meaningful conversation. By the third day he felt the discomforting itch of heat rash in his crotch, the new diet was already causing bowel troubles, and during the last night of the patrol, the first monsoon rains fell, leaving him drenched and his bedding completely soaked. He was not unhappy when the Dai Uy ordered the boats to return to Ha Tien.


When they arrived back at the naval base, Alexander gathered his gear and walked to the administration building with the Dai Uy, who put his hand on Alexander's shoulder.

"You will like," assured the Dai Uy. "Patrols are number one." With a grin, he shook Alexander's hand and stepped into the Quonset hut.

# Chapter III

"Well if it's not the returning warrior," Holloman greeted Alexander. "Three days on the river and you already look like a war casualty. How'd it go? Get into any shoot-em-ups?"

"The only battle was with the mosquitoes. Goddamn, Holloman, this could be a long year," Alexander said with a sigh.

"Too bad we couldn't have the ladies at the Crazy Horse perk you up with a massage and a hot bath," Holloman joked. "Nothing here but gnats and *nuoc mam*."

"Have you seen Sanchez?" asked Alexander.

"He's probably at his girl friend's house. Sanchez has been living with a slant-eyed dumpling for the last couple of months," Holloman said. "Don't know if it's against navy reg's or not, but I'm all for it. Looks like my group goes out tonight. Both the 43 and 44 junks are leaving after lunch. Something must be brewing."

"Three days are *beau coup* for me. Number ten,"

said Alexander, easing himself onto his cot.

"Looks like you'll be here by yourself for a couple of days. Westy headed back to the real world. He left for stateside yesterday. His replacement won't arrive for a week. I scrounged a few books from the support ship. Also got us another radio, so you can monitor our calls. When you get a chance, would you put up some ceiling fans and drapes?" quipped Holloman.

Alexander did not hear Holloman's last remark. He had already fallen asleep, still wearing his boots.

A few hours later he was awakened by Sanchez shaking his foot. "Excuse me, sir. I need to take the radio and Starlight scope. We're leaving for patrol soon. How was your first trip upriver?"

"Fine, fine," replied Alexander, still half asleep. "Let me shave and I'll walk down to the base with you."

The nap had relaxed him, although the heat rash had now spread to his underarms. He grabbed part of Sanchez's gear, and the two walked from the advisor's compound down the hill toward the base.

"Holloman tells me you live here in town with a girl," said Alexander.

"Yes."

"Is that safe? What if some VC wants to blow you away?"

"No place is safe from that, at least not in Ha Tien," answered Sanchez.

Alexander sensed that Sanchez was not interested in any further discussion about the subject, but he wondered if he shouldn't insist that Sanchez move back to the advisor's quarters. Right now, though, he wasn't going to pass judgment. Too many other concerns took priority.

"Holloman thinks something is brewing," said Alexander.

"Yes, sir," said Sanchez. "The Dai Uy says we're going to invade Cambodia."

"Invade Cambodia? You're kidding me. How the hell would the Dai Uy know that?"

"He's usually right," responded Sanchez.

What a goddamn war, Alexander thought. Here I am, stuck with worn-out boats and weapons that were obsolete twenty years ago, and I'm supposed to advise a Vietnamese counterpart who knows tenfold more about what's going on than I do. Not to mention, we only have air and artillery support on one side of the goddamn river.

The customary bristle of activity at departure was underway. Feeling slightly culpable that he had three days off while his counterpart had only a half-day turnaround, Alexander passed a few brief words with the Dai Uy. The Dai Uy was enthusiastic, barking orders at the various junks. He must truly enjoy river operations, thought Alexander, as he handed the Starlight scope up to Sanchez.

"Well, keep her in the road, Sanchez," he said.

A smile spread below Sanchez' wispy moustache. "No problem. Number One."

In no time the junks were crossing the shallow muddy harbor like runaway dogs headed for the mouth of the river.

The next morning Alexander called for a helicopter pick-up. Fifteen minutes later he was sitting next to the wing gunner of a Huey 2B looking down at Ha Tien Bay. Its ginger brown water extended for miles into the Gulf. It's no wonder they call us the brown water navy, he thought. Two miles offshore he saw the familiar haze-grey of an American ship, the USS Garrett County LST-786, base support ship for the U.S. Navy's PBR and Swift boats and Seawolf helicopters.

Alexander was surprised to find onboard an old friend, Lieutenant Pete Silver. After escorting Alexander to the wardroom and listening to Alexander's request, Lt. Silver summoned the two Seawolf pilots. Both assured Alexander they would assist the Vietnamese junks anytime he needed them.

"Do you ever give fire support to the west bank of the river?" Alexander asked, intentionally avoiding the word Cambodia.

"The Whiskey bank? You bet. If you're in deep shit, we'll follow your tracers," replied one of the pilots.

Alexander was delighted to learn that the rigid policy of forbidding air support into Cambodia could be unofficially bent at the level that really mattered.

"If you ever need anything from the Vietnamese, like *nuoc mam* or betel nut," he told the pilots, "just give me a call. That's about all we have to offer."

"Thanks but no thanks," smiled one of the pilot. "We like the food aboard ship."

Alexander spent the rest of the day meeting with PBR and Swift boat drivers who patrolled the river. He was invited to eat dinner in the wardroom. The standard shipboard meal of corned beef and cabbage, fresh baked bread and peach cobbler reminded him of how far removed his life onshore was from the regular ship's Navy. He admitted he missed the Navy food.

After the meal one of the PBR drivers offered to take Alexander back to Ha Tien. As soon as he stepped aboard the small fiberglass boat, the PBR driver opened the throttle and whisked away from the ship. The power and speed of the craft was impressive. This one small river patrol boat could out fire, out maneuver, and out run any three of his old junks. The PBR dropped him at the foot of the promontory and roared off toward the river mouth.

The Coastal Group 43 boats returned to Ha Tien after six days on patrol. Only the 44 boats were left upriver. Both coastal groups lagged their day back in Ha Tien so that junks were on patrol at all times, giving each coastal group one day off every six days.

Alexander met Sanchez at the docks when the 43 junks arrived. As they left base and walked past the entrance, a strikingly beautiful Vietnamese girl dressed in a traditional *ao dai* approached them. Sanchez reached for her hand.

"Lieutenant, this is my girlfriend, Tho." Tho

looked toward the ground, hesitating before she accepted Alexander's outstretched hand.

"It's nice to meet you," Alexander said, trying to put her at ease. No wonder Sanchez speaks Vietnamese so well, he thought. A dictionary like that would improve anyone's vocabulary.

# Chapter IV

The next afternoon the 43 boats left the docks later than usual, just at dusk. Four of the junks towed sampans. When they reached the river mouth the Dai Uy motioned for Alexander to join him in his cabin. "I bring sampan," the Dai Uy explained. "Tonight we ambush VC for sure. You have radio and Starlight scope?"

Alexander nodded.

"We move upriver and spread far apart. Put sampan between junks. We catch VC crossing river," assured the Dai Uy with a grin. A tremor of adventure showed in his face. "You and me go in sampan," he continued. "We stop boats soon. Lots of mosquitoes here. VC don't like mosquito, but maybe VC afraid of Navy more than mosquito."

The junks pulled over one-by-one along a two-mile stretch of the river on the Cambodian side. Each tied up to the thick undergrowth only a short distance from narrow canals that intersected the river. Alexander marked their locations on his map and called in the coded positions to NOC.

A sailor pulled the empty sampan alongside the junk. Carrying his radio and an M-79 grenade launcher, the Dai Uy stepped into the small, narrow boat. Alexander followed, encumbered with the Starlight scope, his radio, M-16, and several cartridge clips. Two more sailors joined them in the sampan, which reduced the freeboard to less than an inch. One of the sailors carried a 57 mm recoilless rifle which was shoulder-fired, like a bazooka.

They quietly cast off from the junk and guided the sampan downstream until the Dai Uy motioned them to tie up less than a hundred feet from the mouth of one of the small intersecting canals. Across the canal the land was open and flat, providing a good field of fire.

Mosquitoes descended in earnest, covering Alexander's exposed skin. Sanchez had told him the Vietcong could smell mosquito repellant, so he had not applied any to his face or hands. A substantial mental effort was required to endure the persistent insects.

The sky was overcast, a starless bowl. The air was still and tepid. The only sound was that of coughing sailors aboard the junks. Alexander suddenly understood how easily the Vietcong could locate the junks' positions: by simply approaching the river and waiting for the telltale sounds of coughing. He turned on the Starlight scope and scanned the Cambodian shore. In shades of light green he could see far into Cambodia. Across the opposite bank in

Vietnam were two granitic peaks where the U.S. Army stationed 105 mm forward artillery bases. The quiet peacefulness of the river soon lulled him into a fitful doze.

The Dai Uy lightly tapped Alexander on the shoulder and pointed to the Cambodian side of the river. Instantly alert, he scanned the flat horizon with the Starlight scope, but he saw nothing. Then he heard a cough. That's not from our junks, he thought. He fumbled at the switch on the Starlight, apprehensive that the instrument's high-pitched whine would be detected. He scanned the flat horizon in front of their sampan, and still saw nothing. Quietly the Dai Uy cocked and loaded his M-79 grenade launcher. All in the sampan stared into the inky night toward the sound of the cough. Maybe, thought Alexander, we'll catch the VC by the same means that they avoid us.

Looking through the scope Alexander saw, less than a hundred yards away, shadowy forms moving toward the river. He quickly handed the Starlight to the Dai Uy, who took one brief look and clicked his radio transmitter button twice.

Now Alexander could discern six shadowy figures moving along the canal bank next to the tree line. Two of them were pulling a sampan in the canal.

"Pop."

Abruptly the night was illuminated by the Dai Uy's flare, who had repeatedly cautioned his men not to fire until they saw the flare. Most ambushes were unsuccessful, he told them, because they were prematurely triggered. As soon as the flare lit the night, the Dai Uy fired a round from his M-79. The grenade exploded close to the moving figures. Instantly tracers flashed from the boats as the junks poured in .30 caliber and .50 caliber machine gun fire.

The noise was deafening. Without any warning the sailor on the back of their sampan fired the 57 mm toward where they had seen the VC. Its recoil nearly flipped over their small sampan. Alexander's heart was pounding; his mouth was dry. He fired off an entire clip from his M-16 toward the tree line without even aiming. The radio, he remembered, use the radio! He shouted into the transceiver for the Seawolves and spilled off his position, forgetting to use the KAK codes.

"Roger. We'll be there in a few minutes. Hold 'em down," answered the voice calmly over his radio.

More red tracers coming from different angles lit the night in the direction of the grenade burst. Alexander saw green tracers coming toward their sampan. His heart was pounding loudly as he ripped off another clip from his M-16. "Hurry up, goddamn it!" he shouted into his radio. The noise of firing blotted out any reply.

Within minutes the two Navy helicopters were overhead and began spraying the tree line. Each chopper carried two 7.62 mm mini-guns that could fire 3600 rounds per minute, a door-mounted M-60 machine gun, and a pod of 2.75 inch rockets. Red tracers from their mini-guns looked like a deathly red, moving hose. A 2.75 inch rocket landed on the Cambodian bank and exploded in an ear-splitting burst of white light.

"Alpha Lima, this is Sierra Tango." The voice was calm and detached. "Better get your junks into the middle of the river. We'll take over from here." Ricochets from the helicopters enveloped the boats.

"Dai Uy," Alexander shouted, "tell the boats to get in the middle of the river! *Di di mau!*" He pointed for them to get to the middle of the river. "*Di di mau!* To the middle!"

The Dai Uy nodded. He understood. His expression showed both delight and anxiety as he gave the order over his radio. Soon the helicopters were making a second run, this time firing on both sides of the river. Their sampan seemed to be consumed by the deafening, formidable firepower of the helicopters. After a third and fourth run the choppers abruptly ceased firing and rapidly gained altitude.

"Alpha Lima, that's it. What were we shooting at, over?"

"We caught Charlie crossing the river," answered Alexander into his radio handset. His adrenalin was still pumping. He started to explain in greater detail, but decided against it. "Hey, thanks a million. Jesus, that was awesome."

"All in a day's work. Anyone hurt? Need a medevac?" asked the pilot.

Forgot about that, Alexander mumbled. "Dai

Uy, is anybody hurt? Any sailors wounded?"

The Dai Uy spoke into his handset, waited for the reply, then shook his head and yelled, "Number one. Nobody hurt!"

"Sierra Tango, this is Alpha Lima. We're all right down here. Thanks for the assist."

"No sweat, man. We'll be heading back now. Enjoyed the fun. Give us a call anytime. Sierra Tango out." The whap-whap-whap of the choppers' blades receded into the dark night, leaving behind an eerie silence.

"Tomorrow we take marines and make sweep," said the Dai Uy quietly in Alexander's ear. "Tonight no more VC, only mosquitoes. Seawolf number one. Maybe scare away many VC. If too many VC, they kill us. But not tonight, you understand?" He grinned.

Alexander nodded. The lesson of superiority of firepower was forever engrained in him, no matter that thousands of bullets had been expended to eliminate what appeared to be only a small squad.

"Yes," Alexander replied softly. "Seawolf number one."

The language barrier precluded any further verbal communication, but they both understood each other clearly. Alexander was pleased with the Vietnamese sailors, even though they had received little or no return fire. The key to a successful ambush, he had been told, was the element of surprise. Now he knew what that meant. Who surprised who determined who won and who lost. Ambush might be the world's oldest form of warfare yet in this world, he thought, I also want to be on the side of superior firepower.

A gentle rain began falling. The sailors huddled in the sampans and in the junks the rest of the night, thoroughly soaked by the rain, but at least they found a dubious relief from the mosquitoes. Finally, with first light, the Dai Uy called on his radio for the sampans to return to the junks.

Breakfast was ready. Alexander wolfed down the hot rice and spicy crab soup with relish. Rain continued to fall in a steady drizzle. The Vietnamese sailors seemed unconcerned — rain was as natural to them as sunshine. The talk was animated because of last night's ambush. Soon the Dai Uy was on the radio again, and within minutes sounds of the junks' motors filled the air and the Vietnamese marines began putting on their flak jackets and combat boots. The junks lined up single-file behind the Dai Uy's boat and headed downstream toward the small canal where the ambush had occurred.

The marines quickly disembarked. Once onshore they formed a sweep line and began searching the shredded Cambodian bank. The foliage had been stripped by shrapnel. Rockets had left craters and gaping holes. The Dai Uy motioned for Alexander to follow and bring his radio.

Alexander kept his eyes pinned to the ground. He knew that a majority of the U.S. casualties in Vietnam had been from mines and booby traps. Walking became awkward a few feet beyond the

59

river's edge as his boots sank ankle-deep into the mud. What a great place for a sucker punch, he thought. Here we are on Cambodian soil, out of artillery support, probably twenty minutes from any help from the Seawolves, and nothing but a mud pit to hide in.

A shout came from one of the marines. He followed the Dai Uy to a clump of thick undergrowth. There, lying face up in the blood-soaked mud, was the body of a dead Vietcong. A bullet had clipped the top of his skull. Its impact had forced rice out of his mouth, nose, and ears. Alexander stared, jolted by the sight. Repulsed, he turned away.

After another hour of trudging through the mud and finding nothing, the Dai Uy ordered the troops back to the junks. One sailor dragged the body of the dead VC behind him while another proudly carried the victim's AK-47.

Alexander kept picturing the image of the dead VC. The soldier could barely have been seventeen years old. Alexander watched while the Vietnamese soldiers tied the dead body spread-eagle to the bow of the junk. Before the sailors finished the task, the Dai Uy ordered the junks to move to the Vietnamese side of the river.

The Vietnamese bank was heavily overgrown with brush and palmetto. The troops began another sweep along one side of a small cross-canal that intersected the river. The rains had stopped, and now the heat and humidity were stultifying.

"*Crumpf!*"

A sudden explosion not far away sent everyone face down into the mud. Alexander was confused. His first thought was that a mine had been detonated. The Dai Uy was shouting at him and pointing to his radio.

Alexander suddenly recalled the dufflebags with seismic sensors to detect movement on the Vietnamese side of the river. "Shit!" he muttered. "We're under attack by our own goddamn artillery." He pressed his radio transmitter. "November Oscar! November Oscar! This is Alpha Lima." His voice was shaking. "105's are hitting our position. This is an emergency."

A second explosion landed, this one much closer. The Dai Uy jumped up and started running and shouted for the others to follow. He rapped Alexander on the helmet and scurried headlong through the thick growth. Alexander rose from the mud, stumbling after him, and nearly fell headlong into a narrow canal, which the Dai Uy and the others had jumped into for protection from their own artillery.

Alexander grabbed his transmitter again. "Goddamn it, answer me!" he shouted. "Tell the Army to cancel their firing. They're hitting friendlies. Jesus H. Christ!"

"What's your location?" The voice was detached.

"Hold one." Alexander scrambled for his map, which he kept folded inside his flak jacket as a third round landed right where they had been standing when the first round fell. He hurriedly gave the coordinates over the radio.

"The artillery has been cancelled. Sorry about that. It was a com problem with the Army."

"A com problem. You call this a com problem?" shouted Alexander angrily.

"I guess they didn't get the message. Sorry."

"Sorry, my ass," sputtered Alexander. He slammed down the radio. Un-goddamn-believable. Gross fucking incompetence. His legs were quivering. The Dai Uy pulled himself chin-deep in the muddy water next to Alexander.

"Alex, you forget to call our position to Army."

"No, I did not forget, Dai Uy. I called the Navy. *They* forgot to call the Army, or maybe the Army forgot to tell their artillery. I am sorry."

"No worry. Now we know how VC escape," he grinned. "He get in little canal." The Dai Uy's eyes sparkled.

He must like this shit, thought Alexander.

The Vietnamese sailors began pulling themselves from the canal and started stripping down. Alexander winced when he saw slimy, three-inch leeches attached to their bodies. The sailors lit cigarettes and, laughing like children, began burning the ugly creatures until they dropped. He looked down and saw a half dozen leeches attached to his own legs and belly, small rivulets of blood forming at their mouths. The Dai Uy handed him a cigarette and, with a grin, indicated for Alexander to burn them off.

"How you say in English?" asked the Dai Uy, pointing to a leech.

"Leech. Leech."

"Lich, lich," repeated the Dai Uy. He then removed one from Alexander's back, held it up like a prize and smiled. "Lich, lich."

"How you say in Vietnamese?" asked Alexander.

"Dia."

"Dia," repeated Alexander and smiled back. Is this funny, he thought.

For two more hours they marched through ankle-deep mud among the dense brush and nipa palms along the Vietnamese side of the river. Charlie had long abandoned the area. The heat became unbearable as battalions of mosquitoes swarmed around their heads and hands. By the time the Dai Uy called to return to the boats, Alexander was exhausted.

After two more days on the river the junks finally headed back to Ha Tien. Alexander was happy to spot Holloman standing at the dock, his sweat-stained Australian bush hat rising above the crowd.

"Well, my friend," said Holloman to Alex when the junks finally shut down their engines. "We heard about the ambush."

"Quite a trophy we brought in," replied Alexander, pointing to the boat with the dead VC strapped to its prow. "Wonder what the taxidermist will charge? Just like a trophy deer. The only difference is the objective. Doesn't the damn thing stink, though?"

"You said it," said Holloman. "Come on, let's

have a beer at Ong Minh's"

"Is Sanchez around?"

"I haven't seen him today. He usually comes up to the advisor's house every afternoon, but I imagine he's making hay with his sweetie. Have you seen her yet?"

"I met her before we went out."

"Now that's something worth fighting for. Piss on Asian democracy and containment of communism. Gook poontang — now that's a worth fighting over."

Alexander couldn't help but laugh. "It's just a matter of objectives," he repeated.

For the rest of the day Alexander and Holloman sat in the shade of the lichi trees at Ong Minh's drinking *ba-moui-ba* beer over ice, which had been brought in by boat from Rach Gia that morning. After several beers, Holloman's growing cynicism surfaced.

"Listen, Alex, the problem with Vietnam is this is a *limited* war. The politicians tell us we can shoot on one side of the river but not the other. Now what kind of shit is that? How can our government send U.S. soldiers — among them two first-class, home-grown heroes like ourselves — to this armpit of the world with self-imposed rules of engagement that nobody but us adhere to? It's ridiculous. And for what?"

"Somebody has to take responsibility, has to draw the line," Alexander responded. "The U.S. simply can't withdraw into a shell. The world is too small."

"Too small? It's too *big* to protect every regime that screams for help. What's our strategic objective here? Do the gooks give a flip? They can't read or write. They squat to shit, squat to cook, squat to eat. They could care less about communism. Squatting and eating and screwing, that's all they care about. And they've got it right. *We're* the ones with the screwed up objectives."

"You're beginning to sound like the campus protestors at home," rebuffed Alexander. "If there's one thing Americans take for granted, it's our freedom. In my book freedom is still worth fighting for, even if we have to do it here."

"Freedom — what's that but a state of mind?" replied Holloman. "In the next limited war the U.S. fights let's hope the national vegetable where we're fighting is watermelon instead of rice. Standing neck deep in a filthy canal on the far side of the world while leeches chew your ass can't be the answer to strategic responsibility."

# Chapter V

The next morning Alexander awoke to the smell of cooking. He didn't remember returning up the hill to the advisor's house. He was still fully dressed and his feet were numb from sleeping in his boots. Dragging himself out of bed, he ambled to the back porch and squinted down at the peaceful village below. Without knowing why, he felt refreshed and happy to be in Vietnam. Sanchez was in the kitchen stirring a dish of rice, shrimp, and duck eggs.

"Good morning," said Sanchez. "How are you feeling?"

"Hello, Sanchez." Alexander opened the refrigerator and poured himself a tall drink of water.

"I heard about the firefight."

"We ambushed Charlie from the sampans."

"That's what I heard," replied Sanchez as he dished his concoction onto a couple of plates. "The other coastal groups will probably start using sampans, too."

"Good. It's the only way to surprise Charlie. The

VC can hear coughing from our junks a mile away."

"A lot of the sailors have TB," said Sanchez.

"What?" replied Alexander. "Tuberculosis?" He was astounded. "On patrol we all eat out of the same dishes."

"Roger that," responded Sanchez without looking up. He put the dish to his mouth and shoveled food in with chopsticks, eating with gusto like the sailors on the boats.

Alexander shook his head in disbelief. Why hadn't they mentioned TB in counterinsurgency school? Was anything they had learned in school relevant? After breakfast, Sanchez took the Starlight scope and the PRC-25 radio and stepped out the back door. The imprints of his boots began to fill with water from the steady drizzle. The monsoon had arrived.

With Sanchez and Holloman on patrol, Alexander was left alone in the advisor's house. He passed the time by replacing worn-out sandbags on the bunker. In the afternoons he walked to the village to buy toiletries. When he passed the food vendors, who now huddled from the rain in thatch-covered stalls, the smell of drying shrimp no longer repulsed him. In fact he enjoyed observing the daily commerce of the central market. In the evenings he prepared his meals on the small propane stove and turned on the extra PRC-25 to monitor the junks' locations, which he then decoded and marked on his map.

On the third afternoon the two Seawolves passed overhead, an unusual event during daylight. He flipped on the radio and immediately heard Sanchez directing the pilots to the junks. The deep *burrp* of .50 calibers sounded in the background.

Alexander keyed the radio receiver. "Sierra Tango, Sierra Tango, this is Alpha Lima. What's happening?"

There was no reply. Either the range was too far or the choppers were too busy to respond. He started to call the LST but decided to keep the air waves clear. There was nothing to do but wait. Finally he saw the two helicopters returning and tried his radio again.

"Sierra Tango, Sierra Tango this is Alpha Lima. Do you read me?"

"Roger, Alpha Lima."

"What happened? Can you tell me? Over."

"Your boats got ambushed," came the casual reply.

"Can you give me a pick up? I'd like to go upriver."

"Our ammo is low."

"I have to get up there. Our advisor was with the boats. He doesn't answer his radio. He may need a medevac."

"Roger, Alpha Lima. We had coms with him until after our first run. Let me check with November Oscar," replied the pilot. When Alexander heard NOC's approval for the pickup. He grabbed his flak jacket and M-16 and ran to the front of the advisor's compound. One of the choppers descended briskly and hovered in front of the advisor's compound. He jumped aboard before its struts touched the ground. Within minutes they were racing upriver toward the ambush site.

From the helicopter Alexander spotted his junks tied to the Cambodian side of the river. Five junks had left Ha Tien. Now he counted only three. When they were high over the boats' location, the chopper abruptly descended and at the last minute flared to a hover above a clearing next to the boats. Quickly unbuckling his shoulder harness, Alexander jumped to the ground.

He spotted three wounded sailors. Two more lay in a heap, dead. He saw no sign of Sanchez. Holding up his palm for the chopper to wait, he franticly helped load the wounded aboard. When he gave the helicopter pilot a thumbs-up sign to depart, the chopper immediately swung its nose down river, skimmed the river's surface until it gained speed, banked abruptly, and ascended above the river at a high speed to avoid small arms fire.

Alexander could hear sporadic gunfire.

"Where is the Dai Uy?" he asked a sailor.

The Vietnamese pointed into Cambodia and made a circular motion with his hand.

Alexander asked where the other boats were. The sailor pointed to the river, indicating that they had been sunk. And Sanchez, what about Sanchez?

"*Co van my, o dau?*" Again the sailor pointed into

Cambodia.

The Dai Uy must have taken most of the sailors on a sweep into Cambodia. Two were left to man the .50 calibers on each remaining junk. Another small group squatted next to the thick brush near the river, smoking and conversing quietly. Alexander ordered them to disperse.

The two dead Vietnamese were piled next to the river, their eyes still open. Their skin already had turned ashen and sallow. Alexander stared at them for a moment, then returned to one of the junks. All he could do was wait.

As dusk faded into darkness a heavy drizzle began falling. None of the normal river traffic hurried home before dark. Somehow the fishermen always knew. After midnight a flare popped half a mile upriver, lighting the sky like a Roman candle. Alexander hoped it was the Dai Uy. One of the sailors reached for a flare to respond but, fearing a trap, Alexander stopped him. In a few minutes another flare popped upriver. Again Alexander refused to respond.

In the pitch darkness, sounds of the river and the drizzling rain became the Vietcong's allies. The chirrup of a frog sounded like footsteps. The whistling wind became enemy signals. Interminably the hours crept by until, as if from sheer exhaustion, the grey light of dawn gradually unveiled their surroundings.

By mid-morning the river traffic had resumed its daily routine, the majority moving downriver to sell their goods at the market. Still there was no sign of the Dai Uy or Sanchez. Two American PBR's stopped at the junks and quizzed Alexander about the previous afternoon's firefight. Alexander's knowledge of the ambush was so limited his answers sounded evasive. It was a comfort to know other Americans were nearby. Their T-shirts were clean and their faces shaved. They had probably eaten a five-course breakfast aboard the LST. Since Cambodia was off limits, Alexander told them not to report the Dai Uy's whereabouts.

"Alex! What you do here?" The shout came from the thick undergrowth. Alexander recognized the Dai Uy's voice. "You think VC shoot us?" The Dai Uy was grinning when he and Sanchez stepped into the clearing.

"Goddamn, it's good to see you!" Alexander called.

"What brings you up here, sir?" asked Sanchez.

"I heard the firefight on the radio yesterday afternoon and got the Seawolves to drop me off. Where have you been? What took so frigging long?"

The Dai Uy grinned and pulled several half-ripe mangoes from inside his flak jacket. "Mango. We go to Cambot to capture mango."

"Mangoes?"

"VC escape. But not mango. *An com* is good today. We make breakfast now." The Dai Uy turned and shouted orders to several Vietnamese sailors.

"So tell me what happened, Sanchez," Alexander demanded. "And what's this shit about mangoes?"

"There aren't any on the Vietnam side," answered Sanchez, as if the statement was self-explanatory. "They say you got the wounded out before night."

"Yes, the Seawolves took three of them back. Those two we left here. So tell me what happened."

"Not much to tell. When our last boat rounded that bend in the river," he said, pointing upriver, "the shit hit the fan. The first thing I see are a couple of B-40's headed at us like burning corkscrews. The next thing I remember is our boat blowing apart. Then I was swimming to shore. We weren't expecting an ambush in broad daylight."

"How many VC do you think there were?" asked Alexander.

"I don't know. We waited to make a sweep until after the Seawolves had sprayed the area. Probably Charlie skipped back into Cambodia in a hurry before the choppers arrived."

"Any VC dead?"

"None that we found. We were pinned down by snipers and lay in the mud all night."

"Did you fire any flares last night, around midnight?"

"Not us."

"Well, thank God you weren't hurt, Sanchez. When we didn't hear your radio, I feared the worst."

"The radio and the scope are at the bottom of the river. If we don't recover the Starlight, An Thoi will have my ass. The Dai Uy says he can salvage the junks."

"How's he going to do that?" asked Alexander, glancing toward the river where two of the junks were already emerging as the ebb tide lowered the river level.

"The Dai Uy called 44 to pick up some empty oil drums at the ARVN base in To Chau. He said he'll use them to raise the boats. We've done it before."

Shortly after noon, two Coastal Group 44 boats arrived. Both were stacked high with the empty drums. Alexander watched with interest as the Dai Uy directed the salvage operation. The empty drums were filled with water, then sunk and lashed to the hull of each junk. A two-handed pump manned by the sailors removed the water from the drums, providing buoyancy to lift the junks to the surface. Alexander knew their Grey marine diesel engines would have to be completely disassembled, cleaned, and reassembled. Luckily the Starlight scope was found wedged between the deck and the gunwale of the Dai Uy's junk.

When the crippled junks, towed by those that were still operable, returned in procession back to Ha Tien, everyone in town came down to the docks to look at the damaged vessels. The Dai Uy seemed to enjoy the commotion.

After offloading their gear and inquiring about the dead and wounded sailors, Alexander asked Sanchez to join him for a beer at Ong Minh's. Spending two days together during the salvage operation convinced Alexander that Sanchez had an exceptional rapport with the Vietnamese.

"Here's to raising the boats," toasted Alexander. They clinked glasses.

"Right. And to finding the Starlight," said Sanchez.

"Sanchez, I'm impressed that you get along so well with the Vietnamese," said Alexander.

Sanchez simply shrugged.

"You speak Vietnamese fluently," continued Alexander. "The Dai Uy and the men obviously respect you as an advisor."

"The Vietnamese don't give a damn about advisors," replied Sanchez.

Taken aback, Alexander asked, "How can you say that?"

"Because I've been here long enough to know. The Vietnamese need advisors for two things. To call in air or artillery support, and to beg, borrow, or steal spare parts for the boats."

"Maybe that's true of some advisors, Sanchez, but not you. The Dai Uy trusts your judgment."

"I've been with the 43 junks nine months," responded Sanchez, "and not once has the Dai Uy or any other Vietnamese asked for my advice. Just leave your radio and Starlight at the docks and see what happens. They don't want our advice. They want our gadgets and our air support."

"You just went on a sweep with them into Cambodia without a radio and without air support," rebutted Alexander. "How do you explain that?"

"The Dai Uy probably figured if an advisor was along and we needed a medevac, the choppers would pick us up, even in Cambodia. Don't underestimate the Vietnamese, sir," Sanchez said with finality. "I better run. Tho will be waiting."

# Chapter VI

On the morning of May 1, 1970, ten days after the daylight ambush, Alexander and Holloman were playing chess on the veranda of the advisor's house when the sound of dozens of helicopters attracted their attention. The sky was filled with American assault helicopters moving across the border into Cambodia.

"Well I'll be damn!" exclaimed Alexander. "This must be it."

"Must be what?" asked Holloman. "Surely we're not invading Cambodia. Charlie will think it's unfair. Would you look at all the choppers!"

For several days the Cambodian invasion was the major topic of conversation among the advisors. Its scale and purpose came in bits and pieces. General Lon Nol had overthrown Prince Sihanouk in a bloodless coup and within days had approved the invasion. Vietnamese ARVN troops spearheaded the drive. American troops were ordered to proceed no more than twenty miles into Cambodia and must return to Vietnamese soil within sixty days.

The Vietcong and North Vietnamese had hastily retreated further into Cambodia. Consequently casualties were light. Huge supply complexes storing millions of tons of rice, weapons, and ammunition were uncovered all along the border. Even VC recreation facilities with swimming pools and tennis courts were found. From the perspective of the advisors, the attack was not an invasion but rather an incursion into an enemy sanctuary. The purpose was not to widen the war, but to remove a grave menace along the border.

"Hey, Alexander!" cried Holloman, holding up a "Stars and Stripes" newspaper. "Did you read this? The National Guard killed some student protestors at Kent State University. Apparently the whole goddamn country is up in arms over what they're calling the Cambodian invasion."

"Where's Kent State?"

"Somewhere in Ohio. Get this. Some pink-o longhairs burn down the ROTC building and attack the Guard. And now the whole country is condemning the Guard for pulling the trigger. They should send the frigging protestors over here to patrol the river. That would change their minds about the invasion. Whose side are they on, anyway?"

"Were the students armed?" asked Alexander, confused at why students would protest an exercise that would shorten the war.

"Armed? What the hell difference does that

make? They were breaking the law, burning down property like a bunch of outlaw vigilantes, and *why*...because Nixon decides to protect our ass by destroying Charlie's R&R camps? What the hell is wrong with America?"

The news of such violent protests was perturbing to Alexander. "Holloman, something *is* wrong. Americans shouldn't be shooting unarmed Americans because of Cambodia. When will this divisiveness end?"

"Only when the war ends, Alex. And instead of coming home as heroes, those assholes will probably treat us, the protectors of their freedom to protest, like a bunch of outcasts. Mark my words," prophesied Holloman, "when we go home they'll treat us like traitors. As if I *want* to be over here. All I ask from life anymore is a good-looking round-eye and a day without the crotch rot."

"Dream on, *amigo*," smiled Alexander. The news from home, though, left him terribly confused and troubled.

PART TWO

# HON TRE

# Chapter VII

Following the Cambodian incursion, patrols became as monotonous as the monsoon rains. Every day rain fell in an unbroken, dreary drizzle. The only diversion came when flocks of fruit bats crossed the river at dusk. The sailors would open fire with automatic weapons on the huge bats, some which had wingspans as large as four feet. The dead bats were promptly gathered, skinned, and cooked in the evening stew.

One rainy afternoon six weeks after their firefight, Alexander was surprised to see the Dai Uy at the door of the advisors' compound. He had never visited them before.

"Dai Uy, what brings you up the hill?" asked Alexander as he opened the door. "Come in, come in." He pointed to a chair. "Would you like a drink?"

The Dai Uy broke into his usual grin and nodded. "Yes. Sure. American whiskey, number one."

Alexander poured his guest and himself straight shots of Jack Daniels. The Dai Uy drank his down in one swallow. Alexander poured him another.

"The big boss tell me we leave Ha Tien," said the Dai Uy, after the second drink. "No more river patrol. Too bad."

"Is that right?" asked Alexander. "What will we do?"

"We move back to home island, Hon Tre, near Rach Gia, maybe one hundred kilometers south. Market Time patrols along coast. Not much activity. Mainly we check ID's."

Alexander could tell the Dai Uy was not excited about the move. "Why do you think we are leaving Ha Tien?"

"After Americans give PBR's and Swift boats to our navy, the big boss don't need junk for river patrol. Before, Americans want junks in river because we are Vietnamese."

The Dai Uy was referring to the recent turnover by the Americans of all the PBR's and most of the Swift boats to the Vietnamese. After the Cambodian incursion, Nixon's program of Vietnamization was being accelerated. Certainly the timing seemed appropriate. No firefights had been reported in more than a month. Alexander had heard that the ship anchored offshore would also be turned over to the Vietnamese. He wondered how the technically sophisticated American boats could be kept operable by the Vietnamese.

"When will we leave?"

"In two days. Tomorrow night we make celebration in the market. You and Sanchez are my guests."

"*Cam on*, Dai Uy," Alexander replied. "We are honored." The news of the shift from river patrols to coastal operations did not disappoint him. Speaking in Vietnamese, Alexander continued, "No more river patrol, no more mosquitoes, yes?"

"In my country you cannot escape mosquitoes," laughed the Dai Uy. "You speak Vietnamese better."

The Dai Uy grinned and finished his drink. "Hon Tre is good", he concluded, "but no action. I see you tomorrow." He rose, shook hands formally, and returned down the hill to the naval base.

As the Dai Uy left, Alexander saw Holloman hurrying up to the compound. He broke the news that Coastal Group 43 would be leaving Ha Tien.

"I came running up here to tell you the same thing," said Holloman. "My counterpart just told me Coastal Group 44 will be re-stationed at An Thoi."

"An Thoi! That's headquarters. Will you be living on the U.S. base?"

"Where else?" responded Holloman. "I don't know if I can readjust to hot showers and an all-American diet, not to mention air conditioning and maid service. How about you?"

"The Dai Uy just told me we're moving to an island called Hon Tre, twenty clicks off the coast near Rach Gia," said Alexander.

Holloman laughed. "Eat your heart out, buddy. While you're dodging hand grenades on some Vietcong-infested island, I'll be tossing down gin and tonics at the An Thoi O-Club. Civilization and flushing toilets, here I come."

"Holloman, you just think you'll like An Thoi. A Vietcong-infested island beats one that's overrun by the brass. You'd better break out the boot polish, you lucky bastard."

"Lord, don't throw me in that briar patch. Can I take three meals a day, ironed sheets, and taps at dusk? *Sayonara*, Ha Tien, and rots-a-ruck to you, Alex. We're leaving this afternoon, so I better pack my gear and run. Come see me when you're at headquarters."

The next evening Coastal Group 43 celebrated their last night in Ha Tien with a banquet held under a parachute canopy spread over a corner of the village market. Most of the sailors had been there more than a year and were excited about the return to Hon Tre. Alexander was seated next to the Dai Uy at the head table, with Sanchez on his right. Many speeches were given, each ending in a toast of *ba-xi-day*, a Vietnamese whiskey which tasted to Alexander like turpentine. In between speeches and drinks a multi-course meal of fruits, soups, shrimp, squid, fish, vegetables, and beef was served. The more the toasting persisted, the less Alexander could understand. The Dai Uy kept plopping choice tidbits from the various dishes into his plate while recollecting events of their river operations. Late in the evening the Dai Uy nudged Alexander and prompted, "Alex, you give toast."

The *ba-xi-day* whisky and festive mood had enervated Alexander. He pushed his chair back and held up his glass. The sailors quieted in expectation. "I am happy to be with you tonight," he said in halting Vietnamese. Then switching to English, "Coastal Group 43 is Number One!"

The sailors roared, and the Dai Uy stood and put his arm around the American advisor. "Good, Alex, good." He then gave a short speech about the American advisors, the *co van my*, which Alexander could not understand, but the sailors yelled their approval.

After the party Alexander staggered up the hill, his head spinning from too much drink. He was pleased, though. For the first time he felt accepted by the Vietnamese sailors for something other than a voice to call in air support.

The next morning the people of Ha Tien gathered by the waterfront to watch the departure of the junks. As the boats cranked their engines and pulled from the dock, everyone shouted and waved. Sailors on the boats tossed colored smoke grenades into the crowd, filling the air with red, yellow, and green smoke. Although the mood was festive, Alexander wondered if the people were sad or were relieved.

"Just like leaving Pearl Harbor with a brass band playing 'Anchors Aweigh'," commented Alexander to Sanchez. They were watching the sendoff from the roof of the Dai Uy's cabin. All their personal belongings were stuffed into two duffle bags. In addition, they had appropriated metal cots and cotton mattresses from the advisors' house. Alexander spotted Tho among the crowd. She looked beautiful. Her raven black hair was pulled back from her head. She was dressed in a pale blue *ao dai*, the traditional dress of Vietnamese women that made them look so frail and feminine.

"What about Tho?" asked Alexander. "You're leaving her in Ha Tien."

"She'll come to Hon Tre when we get settled," Sanchez replied, and then added casually, "we're going to get married."

"Married? No kidding, Sanchez? Well, congratulations!" Alexander extended his had to Sanchez and patted his back. "That's great news." His words did not reflect his doubts.

With a final burst of .50 caliber fire, the junks departed Ha Tien. Alexander wondered what life at Hon Tre would be like, but he wasn't happy they had left the river.

The junks proceeded leisurely down the coast. The Dai Uy was apparently in no hurry to report to Hon Tre. For five days he surveyed their new patrol area, stopping to confer with the village councils at several hamlets along the coast and on the small islands that dotted the Gulf of Thailand. In a manner reminiscent of Captain Cook's arrival in the South Pacific, the boats would pull into a protected cove on an island or along the coast. The Dai Uy and the two Americans would be ferried to shore in small sampans and greeted with ceremonial formality by the village elders. The Dai Uy somberly accepted their hospitality, drank their *ba-xi-day*, and discussed at length what he called, 'activities.' Mainly, he told Alexander, he wanted to assess the loyalty of each hamlet.

The constant, unconscious vigilance that Alexander experienced while on patrol on the river slowly diminished as the junks sojourned through their new Nine Foxtrot patrol area. He and Sanchez took pleasure in simply being in the country and among its people. The shallow brown sea and clear fresh breeze energized his spirits.

The villages were living remnants of an ancient era, untouched by anything but the seasons and the sea. The only evidence of the twentieth century were the ubiquitous Kohler or Briggs and Stratton two-cycle motors that powered the sampans. The more Alexander observed the villagers and their simple existence, the more convinced he became that these rural, island people were not concerned with politics beyond their own hamlets. He doubted that the Vietnamese Navy's reception would have been different had his junks been Vietcong. Basically, the people wanted peace and security, and to be left alone.

On the northernmost part of their patrol area a prominent stretch of land jutted into the brown coastal waters. From the peninsula three granitic mountains rose several hundred feet above the flat coastal plains. The Dai Uy told Alexander that the North Vietnamese were using these mountains, which he called the Three Sisters, as infiltration points for their strongholds further south in the U Minh forest on the Ca Mau peninsula. Landward, the only access to the mountains was either by a well-patrolled coastal highway or down a large coastal canal, both of which were under ARVN control.

The Vietcong, the Dai Uy explained, had thrived in the U Minh forest, which meant the forest of darkness, for as long as he could remember. Although they could subsist from supplies commandeered from nearby villagers, they nevertheless required weapons and ammunition from the North Vietnamese, which were probably carried by small sampans originating from the Three Sisters area. Now that the Cambodian sanctuaries were substantially eliminated, tightening the cordon around the VC strongholds in the U Minh was the next tactical move.

Each morning at daylight, hundreds of boats and open-hulled sampans departed from the villages on the islands and from canals along the mainland to fish in the abundant waters of their new patrol area. Many of the boats dragged nets much like miniature Gulf Coast shrimpers. Some of the larger fishing boats scooped up the fish by pushing nets tied between two long bamboo poles connected scissor-like to the bow. Even ten kilometers from shore the water was seldom more than fifteen feet deep. After one drag of the nets, the boats would empty huge heaps of squirming, flopping sea life onto their wooden decks. The fishermen first culled the undesirable species, particularly the poisonous sea snakes, by discarding them overboard with a short-handled spike. The edible fish, crabs, shrimp, and stingray were placed into separate piles. Prior to dusk the fishing boats returned to the islands, or via the canals to their mainland villages, acknowledging here, as up the rivers, a nightly curfew. Even during the day a three kilometer no-boat zone extending from the shore was enforced.

# Chapter VIII

On the sixth morning after leaving Ha Tien, the Dai Uy pointed the junks to an island that rose from the brown coastal water like a huge turtle, its back humped more than twelve hundred feet above the sea, while its head, a much smaller hill, rose beyond a low-lying neck. The island's total length was no more than three miles; its widest point was less than one mile. One by one the junks pulled into a shallow harbor formed by the turtle's neck, and dropped anchor fifty yards from a sandy beach.

Facing the junks was a small naval base. Two dilapidated tin buildings stood near the shore. Beyond them was a more substantial dwelling with a porch. At the far side of the base on a gentle slope overlooking the bay stood a half-finished house. Its roof was only partially covered, and the side overlooking the harbor was entirely open. A slack, three-strand barbed wire fence, obviously not intended for security, encircled the weed-grown perimeter of the base. In a stand of coconut palms adjacent to the base was a village of thatched houses.

"Well, Sanchez, what do you think?" asked Alexander and continued, "home sweet home, I never thought you'd look like this."

Sanchez raised his eye brows and murmured under his breath, "holy shit."

"Isn't it a beautiful setting? Like a tropical paradise! Dai Uy," Alexander shouted in Vietnamese. "It's beautiful!"

The Dai Uy looked up from the deck at the two Americans on the roof and flashed a smile.

"That hootch up the hill must be our quarters." Sanchez pointed toward the half-finished house overlooking the bay. "It doesn't look too secure."

"Well, we have a great view. Sanchez, we can fix it up, build a sentry tower on the far corner, cut all the brush from the perimeter, string a little concertina, and presto, secure as An Thoi. What do you think?"

"If there's a VC on the island, we're in trouble," rejoined Sanchez. "One hand grenade could wipe out the whole place."

"Alex, come with me," offered the Dai Uy in Vietnamese. "We go ashore to look at the base."

During their trip from Ha Tien, the Dai Uy had spoken Vietnamese to both Alexander and Sanchez. The extra usage had helped Alexander's understanding of the language. He could only understand the tonal differences of the monosyllabic language when the Dai Uy spoke very slowly and with exaggerated intonation.

The entire village must have assembled on the beach to watch the sailors offload their equipment into borrowed sampans. Alexander and the Dai Uy came ashore in the first wave to inspect the base. The sturdy stucco house with a front portico would be used by the Vietnamese officers for their quarters, the Dai Uy told Alexander, and the advisors would live in the half-finished hootch. When Alexander examined their new home, he saw that one wall and half the tin roof was missing, the floor was rotten, and only a few of the windows were screened. Still, he liked its potential and contentedly helped Sanchez haul their gear up the hill to their new quarters. While transferring their mattresses ashore the Vietnamese sailors dropped both their mattresses into the bay.

For the next few days Alexander and Sanchez worked from dawn to dark, cutting the brush from the perimeter, repairing the floor and stairs of the hootch, and filling sandbags to line the inside walls. Sanchez showed Alexander how to dig a defensive trench next to their back door and how to deepen holes at either end.

"If we're attacked, jump into the trench. If a grenade lands in the trench, kick it into one of those holes," instructed Sanchez, "and pronto."

"Where did you learn that trick, Sanchez?"

"After three tours, you learn," replied Sanchez. "With only one year tours, the fellows who rotate out never have a chance to teach their replacements all the tricks. Too many of the new arrivals leave in body bags."

Having repaired everything they could with the limited materials available, Alexander commandeered one of the junks for the twelve hour trip to An Thoi to pick up more building supplies. He returned three days later disgusted and virtually empty-handed. The trip had netted only ten cases of C-rations and one 36-gallon canvas bag for catching rain water.

"The shitbirds wouldn't requisition a goddamn thing," Alexander complained to Sanchez. "Said they didn't have any spare plywood, no tin roofing, and we'd have to get the concertina from the Army. What a bunch of shit-for-brains. Commander Schoen was in Saigon. Holloman was on patrol. The Exec is a short-timer, and the asshole in charge of supply acts like he *owns* the depot."

Sanchez was not surprised.

"We've got to come up with Plan B," continued Alexander. "Without plywood and tin roofing, this hootch isn't worth a shit. You got any suggestions?"

"I've already talked to a carpenter in the village about building a house for me and Tho. We could build a bigger house and all three of us live in it."

"Live off base?" queried Alexander. The thought was intriguing.

"It's probably safer. The base is nothing but a target."

"I think I like the idea," said Alexander. "Let me talk to the Dai Uy. If he doesn't care, let's do it. We'll go native. Build a thatched house, get us some pigs and chickens and a bunch of dogs." The more he thought about it, the better he liked it. "Great idea, Sanchez! We'll go native."

The thought of living in the village completely replaced his anger at the lack of support from An Thoi. On the island, self-sufficiency was the only dependable alternative.

The next afternoon Alexander and Sanchez met the carpenter at the local bar. For the price of several rounds of *ba-xi-day* and $90 U. S. military script, they negotiated a deal for a small plot of land on the slope of the mountain, abutted against two large granite boulders just above the village. The cost included the building of a thatched house with three rooms and a concrete floor. The carpenter solemnly accepted the down payment with a flimsy handshake, and before starting work, spent two days at the bar getting drunk with his construction crew.

The schedule for coastal patrols was easier than river operations. Market Time patrols only lasted forty-eight hours, followed by three days at Hon Tre. The two advisors had the third day together on the island.

As soon as he found the time Alexander took one of the boats to Rach Gia, the closest mainland city and a bustling commercial center, provincial headquarters for Kien Giang Province. In Rach Gia he met with the Naval Intelligence group and received instructions on the new KAK codes, and arranged where his and Sanchez mail was to be sent. He was pleased to discover a U.S. Army battalion headquarters that had an open galley for all Americans. With reasonable support from Rach Gia, island living could be neither completely isolated nor too primitive.

In two weeks the thatched house was completed. The village carpenters had hand-sawed the framework planks from large trees, shaped them with an adze, and pegged and lashed them together without nails. The thatch roof and sides were woven in one day. The simple floor plan had two bedrooms in the back, and one larger living room in front. The roof was shaded by several coconut palms. From the porch they had a splendid view of the bay.

Sanchez acquired two pups, one he named Bourbon and the other Junior. The advisors hired a one-eyed cook to prepare their meals and handle their laundry. The retina of the cook's blind eye was blue, which Alexander said was a sign of good luck.

The one-eyed cook turned out to be talented. Whether shrimp or duck eggs, stingray or crab, he concocted dishes that were appetizing and savory. Rice accompanied every meal, yet the variety of vegetables was exceptional, and entirely seasonal. Except for a small generator at the base office, the island was without electricity. Therefore when tomatoes were in season, the cook used tomatoes in every salad and soup or mixed them with fish and aspic. During ginger harvest, the shrimp and fish were always spiced with various ginger recipes. When stingray was abundant, they ate stingray every day, prepared in a variety of tasty recipes. *Nuoc mam* complimented the dishes perfectly. Alexander, like Sanchez, enjoyed dipping all the dishes in the pungent perhaps putrid fish sauce. When he had first arrived in Vietnam, the sauce had made his stomach churn.

One evening not long after they had moved into their new thatched house, Alexander had a thought. "Sanchez, let's throw a house warming party". He had been on the porch with Sanchez, enjoying the view of the bay after an excellent meal prepared by the cook when it occurred to him to throw a party.

"Here we are, Sanchez, living like kings in a tropical castle. I think we should feed the whole goddamn village. What do you think?"

"It's not like they don't know we're here," Sanchez responded.

"I'll go into Rach Gia and pick up some T-bones and Irish potatoes," said Alexander. "The rich food should give our little amigos a good case of the Ho Chi Minhs. What do you think?"

Sanchez smiled. "Maybe we should feed them cheese sandwiches. They're so used to diarrhea, a reverse dose of the Ho Chi Minhs might be a better choice."

The Dai Uy was amused with the idea. With his approval, Alexander left early the next morning for Rach Gia to pick up a dozen cases of frozen steaks and enough potatoes to feed the village. Back on the island, Sanchez rigged a makeshift grill. By the late afternoon the steaks were sizzling on the grill. While they cooked, the two Americans listened to a battery-operated radio blaring loud, dissonant Vietnamese music and drank *ba-mui-ba* beer over ice that was occasionally brought to the village from Rach Gia.

"That music drives me nuts," admitted Alexander. "It's so damn awful, I'm beginning to like it, which is sure enough a bad sign. Anyone who likes *nuoc mam* and Vietnamese music has a cultural problem."

"I can't stand it either, even after two and a half years of eating rice," said Sanchez. "Why don't we turn it to a gringo station?"

"No way, *amigo*. Tonight we're going native. I told the Dai Uy to show up about dark. Here he comes now."

The Dai Uy was decked out in full dress uniform and formally shook hands with Alexander and Sanchez. After his arrival several other sailors trickled in, and soon the entire house and surroundings were packed with sailors and villagers. The food was consumed in short order. Since there weren't enough utensils, the locals ate the steaks with their hands. Bottles of *ba-xi-day* whisky were passed around and the talking grew louder and more animated. Several villagers tried conversing with Alexander, however, without the exaggerated enunciation and intonation used by the Dai Uy, he couldn't understand a word.

After a couple of hours the Dai Uy departed, but the villagers stayed on and on. Finally, seeing no end to the festivities, Alexander grew weary and headed to the old advisors' hootch for sleep. Not long afterwards Sanchez showed up, also seeking peace and quiet.

"Whose bright idea was this anyway?" asked Sanchez.

"We can't even sleep in our own house," laughed Alexander.

"Before I left," said Sanchez, "two of our guests got into a fistfight and fell through the wall. By tomorrow morning we may not even have a house."

"What the hell, it was good PR," Alexander sighed. "Maybe if we announce a party every month or so, the villagers won't let some VC chunk a hand grenade at us. End all their free parties, you see. What a crazy-ass war," he mused and rolled over to sleep.

The day after their party, Sanchez left Hon Tre to go to Ha Tien to pick up Tho. Alexander had the damage to their house repaired and left on a two-day patrol. The afternoon he returned, Alexander had cleaned up and was sitting on the porch enjoying the sunset across the bay when he saw Sanchez and Tho climbing the path to the house. It occurred to Alexander that Tho hadn't known about their living arrangements. He suddenly felt some discomfort about the three of them living together, but dismissed the feeling as he walked down the path to meet them. "Hey, Sanchez!" he exclaimed, "welcome home! Tho, good to see you again."

Tho gave Alexander a shy smile.

"How was the trip?" inquired Alexander.

"I need a drink," Sanchez said, shaking his head. Tho immediately offered to go back to the village and bring them both a beer. Tending to their needs seemed to make her more comfortable.

Sanchez dropped Tho's small bag in their bedroom, then joined Alexander on the porch.

"Well, how was the trip, Sanchez? Tho looks great. It's good to have you back."

"What a damn three days," sighed Sanchez. "When I left the island on the 3 a.m. water taxi to Rach Gia, it was full of pigs for the market. The seas were so rough the pigs got sea sick. We arrived an hour before sun-up, so I couldn't leave the filthy-smelling water taxi because the civil police would have shot me for breaking curfew. I hitched a ride on a motor scooter to the Rach Gia airport, and had to wait six hours to catch a chopper to To Chau. When I finally got to Ha Tien, Tho's family was in hysterics because their daughter was leaving home with a worthless foreigner. And then on the drive back to Rach Gia the bus broke down twice. It was a great trip."

Alexander clapped his hands and laughed. "Seasick pigs?" he repeated. "I'll bet that was lovely. What a nice trip. At least you brought Tho back. I hope she doesn't mind our living arrangement."

"She's fine with it. She's lived in a smaller house with half a dozen family members."

"Speaking of pigs, Sanchez, meet the new pet. I named him Oink Johnson." Alexander pointed to a sway-back, runty shoat that was sleeping next to the porch. "He started following me around."

"What the hell do you want with a pig?"

"Everybody who's anybody on the island has one," responded Alexander.

The village pigs were not penned, but roamed the beachfront and pathways at will. Large piles of excrement were scattered everywhere, which, together with years of discarded coconut shells, gave the village an unkempt appearance and a distinct aroma. Most of the island's pigs had such sway backs that their bellies dragged the ground. Alexander told Sanchez that one of his future projects was to ask the civic action people to start a pig breeding operation to improve the genetic pool.

"I'll go on patrol for you tonight," Alexander told Sanchez. "It'll give you and Tho a chance to settle in."

Sanchez thanked him and after finishing the beer Tho had brought, Alexander gathered his backpack, flak jacket and gear for the patrol, and trod down to the Navy base. The runty, sway-backed shoat rose and, with a dissatisfied grunt, dogged his heels.

# Chapter IX

When Alexander boarded the junk, the Dai Uy was waiting for him. "Alexander, look at this," he said in English. The Dai Uy handed Alexander a note. It had been discovered by one of his sailors in a hollow length of bamboo on front of a house adjacent to the base. The torn piece of paper had writing on both sides.

"What does it say?"

The Dai Uy translated.

> "My name is Thanh — everybody calls me Hen. I have ordered Comrade (Cong tac) Tranh — everybody calls him Hung — to come to Hon Tre for activities (hoat dong). Cong Tac Tranh is to accept (that hoi) a few good men, but not obligate them. On 7 August send every mission/activity quickly to me. Dong Chi Huyen — everybody calls him Hao — will

*come on August 20 and our mission must be in place by then. From Zone (khu) I to Zone II, III, and IV, especially comrade Huyen must receive a letter."*

"What does it mean?" asked Alexander.

"VC wish to observe our activities at Hon Tre," the Dai Uy said.

"Do you think they will try to overrun the base?" Alexander pictured how easily that could be accomplished.

"No. It say without obligation. But who knows?" He grinned.

Alexander pondered the note for a few minutes, then asked, "Dai Uy, who are the VC? We never see them. Yet they must be everywhere, even on this island. Who are they?"

The Dai Uy was perplexed by Alexander's question. "They are the enemy. They kill my family and cause the war to continue."

"Yes," said Alexander, "but who *are* they?"

"They are bad people. Maybe," the Dai Uy said and flashed a grin, "you meet VC. Then you ask who he is." This made the Dai Uy giggle.

Alexander smiled, but the thought kept nagging him. He had been sent halfway around the world to fight 'the enemy', and certainly they were his enemy if someone who was trying to kill him and other Americans could justly be called an enemy, but who were they? What were their motives? It seemed bizarre to kill other people whom he knew absolutely nothing about and for whom he had no personal feelings. It was equally strange to be the target of this unknown enemy.

Lying atop the cabin roof that night, Alexander kept thinking about the note found in the bamboo stick next to the base. The fact that it had been found on the island was evidence of how the VC could be present, yet go unnoticed. Anyone in the village, or even one of the sailors, could have left the message. The thought dispelled any chance of sleep. *Who were these guys?*


"Dai Uy, Commander Schoen sent a message wanting to know what we are doing. I think he wonders why we haven't captured any VC." Alexander had received the message from An Thoi via the naval intelligence group in Rach Gia. A month of checking hundreds of fishing boats had resulted in nothing more than the confiscation of a few fake Chieu Hoi amnesty papers.

"My boss talk to your boss," replied the Dai Uy. "Today I receive urgent message to get result."

"What do you think is wrong?"

"I think like on river, VC know where boats are."

"What should we do? We can't hide them on the Gulf."

The Dai Uy flashed a broad smile. "We change patrols. VC intelligence too good. Next patrol we take sampan, like on river. We patrol Three Sisters, close to shore. You and me."

Alexander detected the excitement in the Dai Uy's eyes. During the last month the two had become better acquainted. Unlike on the river patrols, when every moment was taut, the Market Time schedule was easy, even relaxed. During the hot afternoons after their nap, Alexander and the Dai Uy would practice speaking the other's language. The Dai Uy had even become curious about Alexander's volume of Shakespeare and would listen intently while Alexander read from it aloud. Alexander sensed that the coastal patrols were beginning to strain the Dai Uy's patience. After discussing the messages from headquarters, he noticed for the first time in several weeks the Dai Uy's mood was exuberant.

They anchored less than half a mile offshore. One of the granite mountains of the Three Sisters rose steeply nearby, its peak nearly eight hundred feet above the brown sea. Just before dark the Dai Uy confiscated a sampan from an old fisherman, who complained loudly but acquiesced when offered a meal and was assured that his sampan would be returned. Alexander guessed the Dai Uy's intentions. He watched the sun set on a placid sea, the shadow of the mountain lengthening until its opaque silhouette slowly blended into the cloud-covered night.

Shortly before midnight the Dai Uy whispered for Alexander to bring the Starlight scope and radio.

Carrying his own radio and an M-79, the Dai Uy stepped into the confiscated sampan and pulled to life the Briggs & Stratton motor, which cut the night air with its clamor. Because the nightly curfew was in effect, the noise of the small motor stood out like a beacon. Alexander dropped into the sampan. They pulled away from the junk and headed toward the dark mountain.

The sea was permeated by phosphorescent organisms which splashed on the sampan's bow in front of Alexander and left a brilliant, incandescent trail in their wake. Less than thirty yards from shore the Dai Uy shut off the motor. The sampan swung parallel to the beach and, carried by an offshore current, started drifting slowly away from the mountain and down the coastline toward Rach Gia.

Alexander removed the Starlight from its case and began scoping the terrain for any signs of activity. After drifting for fifteen minutes, the Dai Uy quietly dropped anchor. Then they waited. The night was black and forbidding. Occasionally, through a patch in the clouds, Alexander glimpsed stars that seemed to flee from his sight. He inhaled the salty air and sniffed the pungent smells of the nearby shore. Feeling acutely alive, his thoughts paradoxically lingered on his own death. Here it was like another element — wind, stars, sea, earth...and death. Remembering that the sound of a cough could be heard long distances across the water, he muffled his mouth against his arm and sneezed. When the moon broke through the cloud cover, he lifted the Starlight scope from its case and pointed it toward the mountain, which in the reflected moonlight was magnified by the scope and illuminated into shades of green. He felt he could reach out and touch its sinister mass.

From his peripheral vision Alexander caught the flash of a small light. Training the scope in the direction of the flash, he distinctly recognized very close to shore the glowing butt of a cigarette, on the water, moving slowly, quietly along the coast. When the smoker inhaled, Alexander could make out the outline of his facial features.

The man was riding in a sampan near the beach, headed in their direction. No sound was evident, so its motor was muffled. Alexander touched the Dai Uy on the knee and handed him the scope. "VC. Look," he whispered.

The Dai Uy took the scope and after one glance quietly placed a round in his M-79 grenade launcher. Holding the scope next to the barrel, he sighted, and fired. The grenade fell short of its target, but a second round fell close by, forcing the sampan to the beach.

"Alex, call for the Seawolves," prompted the Dai Uy.

Alexander quickly gave the codes for their coordinates to Oscar Lima in Rach Gia and scrambled the Seawolves. Their own sampan was drifting again. After his second shot, the Dai Uy had pulled up the anchor and called in the junks. Both Alexander and the Dai Uy were aware of their vulnerable location, with no cover and very little firepower. The sampan's movement in the current seemed glacial, the moments suspended. All his senses were intensified.

The sound of their approaching junks brought a feeling of relief. When the first junk was two hundred yards from shore, a deep burp of an automatic weapon opened up from the tree line onshore. Green tracers shot past them toward their junks. The .50 calibers and .30 calibers on the junks immediately returned fire and began sweeping the beach with their machine guns. Had the Dai Uy not allowed their sampan to drift, they would have been caught in the crossfire.

From one of the junks Alexander saw the back flash of the 57mm recoilless rifle. He had a mental picture of the scrawny Vietnamese sailor, balancing the weapon on his shoulder and firing at the mountain. No doubt the other sailors were unnerved when the explosion rocked the deck and flames shot out both the back and front of the barrel.

In a short while the Seawolves were overhead. Alexander calmly directed their fire toward the shore where he had seen the muzzle flashes. Curiously, he felt removed from the destruction, an observer, not a genuine participant. Yet he was the one that directed the choppers to unleash their awesome power. The noise from the mini-guns and 2.75 inch rockets was deafening. How could anyone on the receiving end survive, much less continue fighting? he wondered, with a growing fascination at their tenacity. How could the VC withstand such an on-slaught?

"OK, Alex. Good! Good! Number One!" the Dai Uy shouted in English. The fireworks had exhilarated him. "We make sweep in the morning. Number one!"

"Right, Dai Uy. Number one," he shouted back.

Alexander thought of the Navy intelligence boys in Rach Gia, probably now having a drink on the rooftop of their living quarters, watching the distant tracers of his junks' and the helicopters' weapons. Better here than there, he thought. Then the Dai Uy was motoring the sampan to the junks, shouting in his radio not to shoot. Alexander's adrenalin was still pulsing long after he climbed aboard the junk. Nothing, not anything else on earth, could match the excitement of a firefight. Perhaps, he decided later, it's simply a matter of the stakes.

The captured sampan was a VC supply vessel filled with sacks of rice, cases of 80 mm mortar shells, and several ten-gallon casks of *ba-xi-day* whisky. Neither dead bodies nor evidence of blood was found. Because of the proximity to the mountain, which provided an advantageous position for anyone looking down on the junks, the Dai Uy decided against making a ground sweep.

Later that morning Alexander received a call from the U.S. Army asking him to report to battalion headquarters the next time he was in Rach Gia. He wondered what the Army could possibly want. He encoded a radio message to the NILOs, the naval intelligence liaison officers, describing the contents of the sampan and a brief explanation of the fire-fight. Both he and the Dai Uy were relieved that they had interdicted the VC sampan.

Alexander was exhausted when he arrived back at Hon Tre, but the warm greeting from Sanchez and Tho made him feel welcome, and the smell of cooking made his mouth water. Oink Johnson stood to greet him. Tho had cleaned the house as neat as a pin, and the evening meal, prepared by the one-eyed cook, was exceptional.

After dinner Sanchez, Alexander, and Tho sat on the porch, enjoying the tranquility beneath the soft moonlight that reflected from the bay, and cele-brated the successful patrol with vodka and grape soda. When the vodka bottle was emptied, Sanchez and Tho said goodnight and went to their bedroom. Alexander stayed up and scratched Oink's ears and thought about the previous night and what might have gone wrong had the Dai Uy not pulled up the sampan's anchor. The pig grunted in muted pleas-ure.

Alexander finally stood, stretched, and went down the hall to his bedroom, leaving Oink on the porch. He fell onto his bed, tired but content. Just as he was drifting asleep, a sound brought his senses instantly alert. At first he thought it came from out-side the house. Grabbing his rifle, which he always kept beside his bed, he sat upright and listened ex-pectantly. The sounds came from the adjacent bedroom. Through the thin thatch walls he could hear Sanchez and Tho making love. Their bellies in the sultry heat produced rhythmic, sweaty suction sounds. As their passion grew louder, his own sexuality, which he had pushed to the back of his mind, now engulfed him. His discomfort grew as he lay in the empty bed.

After the sounds subsided, he arose quietly, slipped on his clothes, strapped a .38 pistol to his belt, and stepped out the front door. Oink Johnson grunted when Alexander walked past, and dutifully followed him down the path through the village to the sampan that shuttled the villagers and their produce to the water taxi. The larger boat was being loaded for its nightly three a.m. run to the mainland. The pig gave a high-pitched squeal of protest when Alexander boarded the sampan and left him standing in the surf.

Two hours later the water taxi arrived at the dilapidated cement quay in Rach Gia. Alexander immediately jumped to the dock, and, disregarding the all-night curfew, walked briskly two blocks through the darkness to an old hotel on the waterfront. He rang the night bell several times until a withered old Vietnamese security man finally opened the door. The man eyed Alexander suspiciously but allowed the American to enter.

Inside Alexander was greeted by a sleepy-eyed clerk. After a few minutes negotiation, he handed Alexander a key. Alex climbed the stairs to a small, surprisingly clean room, lay down on the bed, and stared up at an ancient ceiling fan. In a few moments he heard a quiet knock on the door. A Vietnamese woman, neither slim nor youthful, entered the room. They briefly discussed business. As she began shedding her clothing, he kissed her while looking into her blank eyes. He pulled her to the bed and gently thrust himself into her softness without caution, seeking some lost feeling of compassion. When morning came he shaved, washed himself, dressed, and left, leaving her asleep on the bed.

# Chapter X

"I'm Lt. J. D. Alexander." Alexander stood before a desk. He was speaking to an army sergeant who obviously waited for further information. "I'm with Coastal Group 43," Alexander continued. "I was told to report to battalion headquarters two days ago."

The sergeant looked over the advisor standing in front of his desk. Alexander's combat fatigues were wrinkled and un-starched, his boots unpolished, his hat non-regulation. "Yes, sir," he responded perfunctorily, and then spoke into a phone before pointing to an elevator. "The Colonel wants to see you, sir. Take the elevator to the top floor. First door on the right."

Alexander knocked on the door of the Colonel's office, hat in hand, wondering why anyone in the U.S. Navy should be reporting to a colonel in the Army. The two service branches never mingled, at least not in his experience. A gruff voice instructed him to come in. The Colonel was staring out the window, his back to the door. He was a short, square-shouldered man with slightly graying hair. In his left hand he held a broken cue stick.

"So you're the Navy advisor we've assigned to the Three Sisters," the Colonel said without turning around.

"Yes, sir," Alexander replied to the Colonel's back.

"Your NILO is supposed to keep me informed on what the hell the Navy's doing in my AO." The Colonel turned and looked directly at Alexander. "But we all know those intelligence boys are a bunch of fucking paper-shufflers. Right?"

Alexander, assuming the question was rhetorical, kept silent.

"Schoen's you senior officer, correct?"

"Yes, sir."

"He's a good man. Had the sense to agree we need to patrol the coast near the Three Sisters." The Colonel began striding back and forth across the room. "This Vietnamization thing is a royal pain in my ass. Already had to turn over half my armed personnel carriers to the Vietnamese, who couldn't keep a goddamn bicycle running, much less a tank. We need American troops to stop the goddamn VC resupply. And what do I get for help? A bunch of goddamn gooks in wooden junks that ought to be used for firewood. Now tell me, sailor, what in the shit are you doing to stop the ex-filtration from the Three Sisters?"

Alexander looked him straight in the eyes,

un-awed but wary. "We captured a VC resupply boat this week, sir."

"Boat! You mean a fucking sampan, don't you Lieutenant? There are three Main Force battalions in the U Minh. That's fifteen hundred men being supplied every week, and you've managed to capture one fucking sampan!"

Alexander watched silently as the Colonel paced back and forth across the room.

"Tell me now, son, how do you think they're resupplying fifteen hundred men right under our nose? There aren't any factories in the U Minh, you know. Nothing even close by to steal. Got to be bringing it in somehow, even though I have a cordon around the whole fucking Ca Mau peninsula, except for the coast."

"Are you asking me, sir?" queried Alexander.

"Hell yes, I'm asking you, *sir*!"

"They resupply in small quantities, probably one sampan at a time, or by bicycle, or small boat through the canals. They can't afford to concentrate their supply chain. After Cambodia, it's too vulnerable."

The Colonel stopped pacing. His lips slightly pursed, his eyes squinted. Alexander had a mental picture of Oink Johnson.

"I know for a fact a lot of their supplies are coming from the Three Sisters. Now, you've got a three click no-boat zone out there, right?"

"Yes, sir."

"Does it do any goddamn good?"

"It leaks like a sieve. Every day, thousands of fishing boats cross back and forth from the mainland. But I think we need it."

"What for, if it leaks like a sieve?"

"It's an excuse to check the boats, and it at least keeps out everyone except the VC."

"Hmmmph. Can your gooks fight?" the Colonel asked pointedly.

"Yes, sir. They like to fight. But they're sloppy at the day-to-day routine of checking for ID's, weapons, Chieu Hoi papers. They aren't efficient, but they like to fight."

"Well, let me tell you what we're going to do," said the Colonel emphatically. "We're going to stop the resupplying if we have to punch a hole in every fucking sampan in the Gulf of Thailand. My choppers are going to start patrolling the no-boat zone, and your boats are going to assist. Is there an advisor on board at all times?"

"Two days out of three, sir."

"You'll need to change that. I'll clear it with Commander Schoen. I want radio coms with your boats twenty-four hours a day, seven days a week. That means an advisor on patrol at all times."

"Yes, sir," Alexander said, without stating how much extra effort the order would require of him and Sanchez.

"Now," the Colonel's forehead relaxed, "is there anything you need? I understand your living conditions on the island are basic."

"Basic is an understatement, sir," Alexander

answered. "We need plywood, concertina, sand bags, and tin roofing. And, I'd like a civic action group to visit the village, and a medical unit."

"Just tell our supply depot what you need," the Colonel replied. "Tell them I said it's OK and to call me personally when they have everything ready for you. You'll have to talk to Commander Schoen about the civic action and medcaps. Now, Lieutenant, here's what I want to accomplish," he continued, looking squarely at Alexander and punctuating his words with two fingers. "I want cooperation, I want information, I want coordination. This is my fucking AO, and I want the VC out of the son of a bitch before we turn it over to the South Vietnamese. Time is of the essence and the Army and Navy will have to cooperate. Every time you're in Rach Gia, come by and report to me personally. I'm looking forward to working with you."

Alexander understood he was dismissed. On the way out he asked the desk clerk for directions to their supply depot. Despite the Colonel's swagger, Alexander was impressed with the results. When he informed the supply staff that the Colonel had sent him, they immediately wrote out a requisition for every item he ordered, which included a gasoline generator, chain link fencing, and extra canvas. They promised the order would be filled and loaded onto a truck within forty eight hours.

With two days to wait, Alexander decided to check in with An Thoi to make certain headquarters had been informed and was in agreement with the schedule change. He hitched a ride from Rach Gia to An Thoi on a Huey 2B which flew close over Hon Tre. From the vantage of the chopper, the island looked just like its description, a sleeping turtle in a dun-colored pond. As they passed its summit, he noted another, smaller village at the base of the mountain along the island's northeast coastline. He could also see, high on top the mountain, small clearings which he assumed were cultivated crops. He made a mental note to scout the entire island at the first opportunity.

When he arrived at An Thoi, before meeting with Commander Schoen he inquired after Holloman. He was told the 44 advisors lived with their Vietnamese counterparts down the road from the U.S. Navy facility. Following directions, he found an un-air conditioned, pre-fabricated cubicle with a hand-scrawled 'Lt. Holloman' on the door. He knocked on the door and looked in.

"Anybody home?"

"Well, kiss a Chinese duck!" exclaimed his old friend. "Look what blew in! Sow the wind and reap yesterday's gas! Come on in to this castle!" They shook hands, and Holloman promptly opened a bottle of Jack Daniels, threw the cap over his shoulder, and handed it to Alexander.

"To sunny South Vietnam," Alexander announced and took a long swig before handing the bottle back to Holloman.

"To my would-be duty station, Big Sur, California and the U.S. Fucking Navy," responded Holloman, who took an equally long draw from the bottle.

For the next few hours they drank and swapped stories. Holloman admitted that he no longer went on patrols since his group now had four advisors. "No sir, no more patrols for this hombre. I let my staff handle the grunt work."

"What the hell do you do all day...lie around this dump and play with yourself?"

"Dump, my ass. It's four hots and a cot. Working showers and USO shows. Shit, man, this is the only way to fight a war. And besides, I go to Saigon regularly. Alex, that place makes Hong Kong and Singapore look like the Church of the Nazarene. Cross my shriveled heart."

"How do you manage to get away?" asked Alexander.

"I just walk my ass to the airstrip and hop a flight. No one tells me I can't, because I don't ask anyone's permission. Remember that Philippine babe in the red dress at the USO show? She's my latest sweet pea. She's shown me places in Saigon that are double-A depraved. Alex, you've got to meet me there. I'll get her to bring a friend."

Alexander laughed. "I don't know about this 'bring a friend' business. I remember that time in Hong Kong when you picked up those two whores..."

"Yeah, I know," interrupted Holloman. "One a slim, almond-eyed beauty, the other a tad on the dumpy side. We flipped a coin for the good-looker, and you got the ugly one."

"And you got the clap," laughed Alexander. "If Schoen would send me another advisor, I'd meet you there, but it's just Sanchez and me. We're on port and starboard patrols."

"Tell you what, Alex. We just got a new advisor last week. He's wet as hell behind the ears. You tell Schoen you need him more than we do. Brooks is his name."

"Hey, thanks, but that means you'll have to go on patrol again. I wouldn't want to ruin your war record."

"Listen, shitbird. Here I am a committed Vietnam warrior confronting communism with my bare hands every single day, and you have the nerve to suggest I'm not pulling my weight? That's worthy of a long discussion over a brew. Come on, let's hit the O-Club!"

The next day Alexander was nursing a throbbing hangover when he reported to Commander Schoen. The commander confirmed that Coastal Group 43 would be coordinating closely with the Colonel on patrols around the Three Sisters. Commander Schoen accepted Alexander's request to transfer one of the Coastal 44 advisors to the Hon Tre group. Brooks would report to Hon Tre in three to four weeks.

# Chapter XI

By the time Alexander arrived back at Rach Gia the water taxi to Hon Tre had already left. He spent the afternoon aimlessly wandering the crowded streets, strolling through the fish and produce markets, looking at the heaps of fish, racks of dried stingray, and pots of live crabs. Vegetables of every kind were spread on straw mats and displayed in colorful stands. Throngs of Vietnamese bargained clamorously. No one paid any attention to him except for the children, who held out their hands for souvenirs. Although he was the only American in the crowded street, he no longer felt ridiculously conspicuous. Weeks ago he had stopped worrying about being attacked by some rabid Vietcong hidden in the urban mob. In fact, he now preferred walking among the Vietnamese rather than purposelessly visiting the American intelligence officers' compound.

Spotting a barber shop, he entered, described in adequate Vietnamese how he wanted his hair cut, and had the man trim his hair. Without feeling any insecurity, he let the barber shave his face and neck with a straight-edged razor, and clean the hair from his ears with a small razor-tipped rod spun between thumb and index finger.

Half asleep in the barber's old-fashioned chair, absorbed into the bustle of daily commerce, he silently questioned if these people really cared an iota about America's effort to stop the spread of communism. The disruption the war caused in the life of every Vietnamese, whether ARVN or Vietcong, city dweller or villager, Buddhist or Catholic, probably made the great majority of the people simply wish for an end to it. With so many hundreds of thousands of casualties, how could there possibly be a claim of victory by any side? He smiled to himself, recalling one of his favorite phrases — in war, there can be no substitute for victory. With his head wrapped in warm towels, he mulled over its validity.

That evening he ate a delectable five-course dinner at a small, brightly decorated Vietnamese restaurant. After the meal he enjoyed sharing shots of Courvoisier and small talk with the smiling restaurant owner. When he left the establishment darkness had fallen and the busy streets were half empty. Before he had returned half the distance to the waterfront, a siren announced curfew. In an instant the streets emptied. The people seemed to vanish in mid-step.

Now what? It was dangerous walking the shadowy streets after curfew. During Tet 1968 the

Vietcong had overrun downtown Rach Gia. Since then, the naval intelligence people told him, the military police who enforced the curfew shot first and asked questions later. No doubt the hotels were locked for the night, and the army's transient quarters and the naval intelligence group's compound were far away near the waterfront. Feeling stupid and exposed, he checked his .38 and loaded a shell in its chamber. The sense of tranquility he'd felt that afternoon was replaced with an uncomfortable feeling of being stalked.

Alexander began walking the dark sidewalks toward the waterfront, pausing cautiously at each street corner. He knew from years of hunting mule deer in West Texas that the quarry was usually found only when it moved. With that thought in mind he took cover in the black shadow of a tall plaster wall that bordered the sidewalk, edging himself along until it recessed at an iron gate. He pressed his back against the cold metal, and slowly dropped into a squat.

Fear didn't grip him so much as a pervasive, agonizing loneliness. He felt like a hunted animal, alone and discarded, half in one world, half out the other. Wrapping his arms around his knees, he stared into a vacant darkness that smelled of urine and stale garbage. Lord, what am I doing here, and for what? He slowly drifted into a fitful sleep.

Alexander was still sleeping when the gate behind him opened, causing him to fall backwards. He immediately rolled sideways, pulled the .38 from its holster and pointed it in the face of a startled old Vietnamese man. Dawn lit the drab overcast sky with a soft light. Heart pounding and half asleep, Alexander stood up, still aiming the gun at the Vietnamese. When he saw that the small man was unarmed, he lowered his pistol and looked around the cobbled courtyard. Two black Citroens were parked near a two-story stucco residence.

"What are you doing?" he asked the old man, who still stood frozen in his steps.

Someone opened the door of the house and shouted in French, "*Ques ca c'est? Ques ca c'est?*"

Alexander stared at a stocky, well-dressed man, then holstered his gun. "I am sorry. I made a mistake. *Excusez moi.*"

"What do you do here?"

"I was returning to the waterfront when the curfew sounded. I fell asleep against your gate."

"American?"

"Yes."

"Where do you live?"

"Hon Tre," Alexander answered. "I am returning to Hon Tre."

"Hon Tre, Isle de Tortoise?" asked the man.

"Yes. I will go now. Again, *excusez moi, s'il vous plait.*"

"Wait," the man said in Vietnamese. "You wish to eat breakfast before you go? Come, join me." He pointed toward the house in a language that anyone could understand.

Alexander started to decline, but he hesitated.

On second thought, why not? The man was only being hospitable. "Thank you, sir. OK." He nodded to the man. "Yes, I will join you for breakfast."

Inside, the house was spacious and cool, the furniture finely upholstered. Exquisite lacquer paintings hung from the walls. His host introduced himself as Mr. Ngong, and asked in faltering English if Alexander would like to bathe before breakfast. Again Alexander hesitated, but then gratefully accepted. A servant led him through a series of hallways to a bathroom and showed him the toiletries and towels.

He closed the bathroom door and inhaled the clean odor of soaps and disinfectants, aromas that he had forgotten existed. Catching a glimpse of himself in the mirror, he stared at his own image and was surprised at his gaunt face. Since his arrival in Vietnam he had lost nearly twenty pounds. That reminded him. Today was the Hump, the half-way point in his year-long tour of duty. From now on he was a short-timer. Jesus, the Hump, he thought.

Alexander ran a tub of steaming water and soaked himself for the first time in months. After dressing and sprinkling cologne on his face and clothes, he made his way to the dining room.

"Do you feel better?" Mr. Ngong stood near the dining room table.

"Thank you, yes" Alexander replied.

"This is my daughter, Thanh," Mr. Ngong said.

Sitting at the table was a young Vietnamese woman who nodded at him without smiling and simply said "*bonjour*". Alexander guessed she was in her early twenties. Her poise diffused a delicate femininity.

"I have asked Thanh to interpret for us," continued Mr. Ngong, "She speaks excellent English. But first, let us eat." He nodded to a servant. Trays of breads and fresh fruits were brought in, followed by marmalade, butter, omelets, and hot tea. Alexander smiled politely.

After he answered questions about where he was from in the United States and eaten his fill, the young woman asked if he would care for anything else. Her English was concise, her grammar was perfect, and he thought her accent was British, or perhaps French.

"No, thank you," he answered. "Please tell your father the meal was delicious, and the bath was especially welcome. I appreciate your hospitality."

The girl spoke to her father, who nodded and replied in rapid Vietnamese.

"My father owns property on the mountain in Hon Tre," she interpreted. "On the mountain top he owns citrus orchards and ginger farms. He said your naval base is on the island. He is curious about the military's interest in Hon Tre. Is there danger of Vietcong activity?"

"No, not on the island," responded Alexander. "We patrol the coast."

She translated this to her father, who again spoke to her in rapid Vietnamese.

"My father says there have never been Vietcong

on Hon Tre," she translated. "It is peaceful and inhabited mainly by Buddhist monks."

Alexander had noticed a few young monks with shaved heads and dressed in saffron robes in the village, but assumed they belonged to a small sect.

"He fears the military will..." She paused as if searching for the second phrase, "...disrupt the peace."

"If there are no VC on the island, your father has no need to worry." Impulsively, Alexander continued. "Does your father know anything about the Vietcong?"

The girl stared at him, her almond eyes unblinking. "He does not know," she said, without waiting for her father's response. Again her father spoke and she translated. "In Kieng Giang Province, the Vietcong have killed many village chiefs. They try to change the...," she searched for the correct word, "...change the *societe*."

The answer added nothing to what Alexander already knew. The longer he was in this country, the more curious he became about this unseen, unidentified enemy. Who *were* the Vietcong?

"Tell your father, if he will come to Hon Tre, I will introduce him to Dai Uy Khuay, who is in charge of the naval base. I am sure the Dai Uy would like to talk to your father. And now I must go. I must catch the water taxi before it leaves the dock. Again, I thank your father for his hospitality."

Alexander rose and extended his hand to Mr. Ngong, and in Vietnamese, thanked him again. He extended a hand to Thanh, and thanked her, too. Her grasp was firm, unlike most Vietnamese.

Alexander walked through the courtyard past the dark green iron gate into the crowded street. When he stepped onto the sidewalk, he turned and looked back to the house, but the door was already closed. The old servant eyed him suspiciously and quickly shut the gate.

The city was again teeming with people and commerce, as if no war existed. It was almost impossible to believe this was the same silent, empty and forbidding city that existed after curfew. As he threaded his way through the crowds and along streets choked with motorcycles and exhaust fumes and dust from trucks and bicycles and pedicabs, he kept thinking of the morning encounter with Mr. Ngong and his daughter. Such a strange coincidence.

Hon Tre was a welcome sight, peaceful as a Gauguin painting. The small island felt like home to Alexander and, like the poem, home was the sailor. He smiled to himself, thinking that Gauguin's paradise probably smelled like pig shit, too. When he approached the thatched house, Oink Johnson rose and, holding its nose high with pointed forward and squinting from nearsightedness, the pig greeted Alexander's arrival with a satisfied grunt.

Alexander entered the house and threw down his gear in the front room. "Anyone home?" he called. Tho stepped into the room.

"Hello, Tho. *Chau co*. Sanchez *o dau*?"

Sanchez was on patrol. Alexander walked to his

room, pulled off his boots, and changed into comfortable black pajamas like those worn by most of the Vietnamese locals. When he returned to the front room he saw that Tho had poured him a glass of lemonade.

"*Cam co*, Tho. God, it feels good to get back."

Tho smiled, and Alexander noted the perfect whiteness of her teeth. "Can you tell the cook I will eat here tonight?"

"Yes," she replied. It was the first word Alexander had heard her speak in English.

"Good. I will visit the Dai Uy. I brought many supplies from Rach Gia."

When Alexander finished the glass of lemonade, trailed by the sway-backed pig he walked down to the Vietnamese officer's house on the naval base. The Dai Uy was in the front office.

"Dai Uy, how are you?" he greeted in Vietnamese. "I have brought many supplies on the junk for the base."

The Dai Uy acknowledged his greeting and pointed for Alexander to be seated. He told Alexander his sailors had already given him the good news. "You have brought a generator, too," said the Dai Uy. His pleasure was evident.

"I think we should give the generator to the village chief to light the waterfront."

"Not use it here on base, Alex?" asked the Dai Uy. "How will village pay for diesel?"

"I can get it from the army. Sometimes I think about the note in the bamboo stick. If we don't help the villagers, maybe they don't help us."

The Dai Uy smiled. "Alex, you worry too much. But OK with me. You bring another generator for the base."

They discussed how to disburse the supplies, and the expectation that more could be forthcoming. On the way back to the house, Alexander stopped at the local bar on the beach, sat down in a chair on the sand under palm trees and ordered a beer over ice. Ice was delivered by the water taxi twice a week, and would last only a few hours. Now that most of the supplies for the base had been procured, he began looking at the village with an eye for improving the villager's lot. A well for drinking water during the dry months would certainly be beneficial. Commander Schoen had promised to send a medcap and a civic action team within the month. As Nixon's Vietnamization program accelerated, the commander had told him, the U. S. military would be emphasizing pacification.

Supper was ready when Alexander returned. The one-eyed cook had prepared a tasty vermicelli and crab soup, delicately stir-fried fish, and a fresh cucumber and cilantro salad spiced with *nuoc mam* and cerrano peppers. Alexander asked Tho to join him, but she declined. When she served the dishes, he could smell Tho's clean, feminine odor. He noticed the shape of her breasts against her blouse. Her waist was delicate and firm, and the contour of her thighs was flawless. Alexander ate the meal in silence. After the cook had cleaned up and left, he tried conversing with Tho but felt self-conscious. He bade her good night and retired to his room, lit a kerosene lantern, and tried to read. Through the thin thatching he could hear her movements as she undressed. Most of the night he lay awake, angry at himself for thoughts which he was unable to douse.

The next day Alexander left for patrol and, halfway to the mainland, met Sanchez' junk returning to Hon Tre. Sanchez shook his head and whistled under his breath when Alexander told him the news about the two of them being on port and starboard patrols.

"But we'll have another advisor here in less than a month," Alexander added. "When he's onboard, the patrols won't be so constant. His name is Brooks. By the way, I'll be moving back to the base as soon as I finish this patrol. We have enough plywood and tin to make the hootch livable. You and Tho need to live alone."

"You don't have to move out. There's plenty of room in the house."

"I know, Sanchez, but with another advisor coming, I'd better move back to the base. Looks like the Dai Uy is ready to roll. I guess for the next few weeks we'll only see each other when we exchange radios and the Starlight." As the junks parted, he waved and called to Sanchez, "Keep her in the road!"


The long November days were hot and oppressive. In the afternoons the sun reflected from the choppy waves like a sea of mirrors. After sunset the stars seemed close enough to touch. One evening Alexander witnessed a full moon encircled by two complete rainbows. Finally, the wind shifted from a wet southerly breeze to a dry northern one. The change heralded cloudy days and windy, cool nights. It was almost, but not quite, a hint of some forgotten autumn, except rather than winter, they now faced six months of the dry season.

The mornings melded into the afternoons, and the afternoons with the evenings. The routine checking of fishing boats became as rhythmic and natural as the swaying of the decks under their feet.

During the day Alexander kept to himself on the roof, reading or daydreaming. After the evening meal he would join the Dai Uy for hot tea in his cabin. The two would talk together in the other's language, Alexander speaking Vietnamese, the Dai Uy replying in English. Most evenings, by the light of a kerosene lantern, Alexander would read aloud from his volume of Shakespeare. He knew the Dai Uy did not understand many of the words or the play's meaning; nevertheless, his counterpart delighted in the phrasing and flourish of expression.

One afternoon when Alexander was napping and the junks were anchored close to shore near the Three Sisters, he was awakened by a loud explosion. Before his head cleared, a second shell exploded within fifty yards of the junk. He heard shrapnel slapping against the wooden planks. In seconds everyone was on their feet. The Dai Uy began shouting orders at the sailors and then into the radio at the other boats. With unusual dispatch, the Vietnamese sailors started the boats, hoisted anchor, and headed straight toward the shore. Their .30 and .50 caliber machine guns raked the lower slopes of the mountain. Several more mortar rounds landed amongst the junks but missed the moving targets by several hundred feet.

By the second mortar round, Alexander had scrambled the Seawolves from Rach Gia. When the helicopters arrived, the junks made one pass along the shore and pulled out of range of the mortars. Once again Alexander was awed by the incredible firepower of the two American helicopters. First they strafed the mountainside with mini-guns, firing a solid stream of 7.62 mm bullets, and then fired off 2.75 inch rockets which blew away entire chunks of the granite mountain. The helicopters received no return fire, and after blasting the mountainside for twenty minutes, turned, signed off with Alexander, and headed back to Rach Gia.

Alexander and the Dai Uy were pleased by the helicopter attack. Being mortared during nap time shattered an unspoken canon observed by the adversaries. That evening they heard a sampan skirting near the shore. Several of the junks fired machine guns in the general direction of the sound, lighting the sky with tracers. After the firing ceased, they could no longer hear a motor, but the next morning found no evidence of a sampan. During the night the Dai Uy moved the boats away from the mountain. A sapper attack was not impossible even a half-mile from shore.

During nap time the following afternoon, while anchored at the same spot as the day before, the junks were once again mortared. Alexander could barely believe the explosions.

"Goddamn, who *are* these guys?" Alexander asked the Dai Uy. He had never witnessed such resolve.

The Dai Uy grinned. As far as he was concerned, the VC were wasting precious ammunition trying to mortar moving boats.

Once again Alexander scrambled the Seawolves and the Seawolves assaulted the mountainside, leaving parts of it smoldering and treeless. Alexander began to ponder, as the rockets exploded against the granite mountain, in a contest between tenacity and firepower, which would eventually dominate.

Back on the island, Alexander spent most of the days working on the advisors' hootch. He moved his personal gear to the half-finished structure, explaining to Tho that he was moving out of the house because another advisor would soon be arriving on base. Now that rain was not a problem, he slept inside the hootch, looking up through the half-finished roof to the starlit sky with only Oink Johnson for company. Except for when he briefly exchanged gear with Sanchez, he neither saw nor spoke to another American for a month.

On one patrol his junks picked up a fisherman

who said he had been captured by the VC and held for two months. The Dai Uy interrogated the man at length, then returned him to his home on a tiny island several miles north of their Nine Foxtrot patrol area. Because the winds were so strong that day, the junks spent the afternoon in the lee of the island. At twilight they returned to a point of land on the mainland called Hon Chong, far north of the Three Sisters.

Not long after supper, two American helicopters began circling the junks. Since his interview with the Colonel, Army helicopters covered their patrol area daily, searching for VC coastal activity. Alexander called to the choppers again and again on his radio. Apparently he did not have their frequencies, and Rach Gia was too far away for radio communications. He stared up at the circling lights and pictured what his junks must look like to the Army pilots, eager to blow away any VC infiltrator. He knew very well how long his junks would survive a mini-gun assault. One of the choppers popped a flare, and the night vanished into a white fluorescent glare.

The Dai Uy joined Alexander on the cabin roof, questioning him with his eyes. When the flare sputtered out, Alexander told the Dai Uy to pop one of their own flares but not to point it toward the choppers. They might mistake the tracer trail as a live round. As the two Army helicopters circled his junk, Alexander felt absolutely helpless. The *whap-whap* of the rotary blades became the sound of impending doom. A raw fear of the American firepower engulfed him. He wanted to shout 'Wait! Hold it! Stop!'

As the two helicopters lined up in a firing run, he grabbed his PRC-25, and again yelled into his radio, pleading that his junks were friendlies, not to shoot. A calm voice responded, "This is Black Pony 47 November, you having some troubles, bub?"

Black Ponies were fixed-wing OV-10 Broncos flown by the U.S. Navy for close air support. Much faster than helicopters, and able to carry the larger Zuni rockets, Alexander had watched them working over targets and had been amazed by their near vertical dives and ability to level off near the ground at incredible speeds.

"Black Pony 47 November, this is Alpha Lima. Two Army choppers overhead are commencing a firing run on us. We're friendlies in South Vietnamese junks. This is an emergency. Over."

There was no response. During the ensuing seconds everyone aboard the junks stared in silence at the circling helicopters. Finally, their tail rotors lazily swung away from the boats and proceeded back toward the coast.

"Alpha Lima, this is 47 November. They thought you were Charlie. Good thing I came along."

"Roger, 47 November. I didn't have their freq's. Listen, a million thanks."

Alexander's knees were shaking and his stomach felt queasy. Never before had he experienced such fear. Face to face with American firepower, he had felt completely overwhelmed by his helplessness.

This, he thought, is what it must feel like to the VC.

In the sleepless hours after the choppers departure, his fear was replaced by anger. He wondered how many American deaths had been caused by the overzealousness of their own troops. In a frontless war with nineteen the average age of the American soldier in Vietnam, the unspoken rule, which he too lived by, was to shoot and ask questions later. How many innocent lives had that cost?

After breakfast Alexander asked the Dai Uy to take him to Rach Gia. The Dai Uy nodded and grinned in understanding. Without the helicopters' radio frequencies, his boats could too easily be mistaken for VC and blown away by the U.S. Army.

The young sergeant at the guard post outside the Colonel's battalion headquarters stared at Alexander in disbelief.

"I said I'm Lt. J.D. Alexander and I want to see the Colonel. Now!"

"Yes, sir." The guard picked up a handset, whispered into it, then looked at Alexander. "Are you Army, sir?"

"Shit, no! I'm senior naval advisor to Coastal Group 43." Alexander suddenly remembered he was dressed in black pajamas like a Vietnamese fisherman. He was bare-headed and had not shaved in two days. "I'm Senior Advisor, Coastal Group 43," he repeated. "Do I have permission to enter or not?"

"The Colonel isn't here, sir," the sergeant responded hesitantly. "He's at his headquarters."

"I thought *this* was his headquarters."

"No, sir, he moved battalion headquarters to the field. This is now a rear post."

Alexander paused, his anger giving way to futility. "When will the Colonel return?"

"He never says, sir. He moves battalion head-quarters in the field nearly every night."

Alexander looked down, his emotions drained. There were two things he could not tolerate — bureaucracy and waiting. He mumbled something to the sergeant, turned and walked out to the street, where he was quickly absorbed by the crowd of Vietnamese peasants.

When Alexander returned to the island that evening, he felt mentally drained. After dinner he drank half a bottle of *ba-xi-day* and poured warm beer in a bowl for Oink Johnson, who slurped it down with gusto. Lying back on the hammock, Alexander spotted an eight-inch gecko which had apparently made its home among the rafters. The large lizard promptly burst into a loud clucking, no doubt a territorial claim directed at the intruder be-low. Alexander picked up his .38 and aimed at the gecko, then slowly put the pistol down. "What the fuck," he mumbled, and clucked loudly toward the reptile before falling into a fitful sleep. Oink con-tentedly snored at his feet.

He awoke at sunrise and looked out the open wall to an orange-flecked bay, so peaceful and bu-colic, and felt completely refreshed. For some rea-son, not controlled by his consciousness, Alexander always awoke in a cheerful mood. The sun also rises, he noted. Another beautiful day in sunny South Vietnam, beautiful as long as you can put both feet on the floor.

"Oink, goddamn it, quit snoring!" he yelled to the pig. "You'll wake the dead. Get up, you damned old alcoholic!"

# Chapter XII

"Someone is here to see you, lieutenant."

The announcement was made in Vietnamese by a young sailor. It was mid-morning in early December. Sanchez was on patrol, and Alexander had spent the morning trying to screen the porch. The hot dry season had set in with a vengeance. The canvas cistern which collected rain from the roof for drinking water was less than half full. Alexander had been experiencing a succession of intestinal disorders, the new advisor had not yet arrived, the port and starboard patrol schedule was becoming tedious and, without another American to talk to, he was downright lonesome.

"Who is it?"

"An old man, sir," replied the sailor.

Alexander strapped on his .38, yelled at Oink to stay put, and followed the sailor down to the entrance of the base. Standing there was Mr. Ngong's old gate guard.

"*Chau Ong*," said Alexander.

The old man barely nodded. "Come with me," he said in Vietnamese with a cracked voice.

"Where?"

"Follow me."

The old man turned, and without waiting to see if Alexander came along, shuffled toward the village. His legs bowed at the knees as though he had carried heavy loads on his shoulders for many years.

With some suspicion, but driven by an over-whelming curiosity, Alexander decided to follow. The old man proceeded quickly through the village without pausing or glancing sideways, and soon embarked on a path up the mountainside. They climbed silently in single file through groves of co-conut palms, past huge granite boulders and, as the slope steepened, through densely matted shrubs and verdant undergrowth. Soon the village was far below them. Now and then they passed small plots of banana trees growing in rows on the steep incline. The small orchards were planted and furrowed but, rather than running across the strike of the hillside, the furrows pointed straight downhill, increasing the erosion they were meant to check.

The old Vietnamese man never stopped to rest or glance back. Alexander was afraid to pause to catch his breath, expecting he would be left behind. More than half way up the mountainside the path widened into a small cultivated plot. When they emerged from the dense foliage the panorama was spectacular. Alexander looked down at the tan water of the Gulf of Thailand, dotted with fleets of small fishing boats. Across the Gulf rose the peaks of the Three Sisters.

The old man disappeared into a thatched house that huddled in a concealed niche next to the clearing. Alexander automatically looked around for cover, noting the excellent field of fire that he stood in. A diminutive figure emerged from the house.

"*Chau ong.*"

"*Chau co,*" responded Alexander, catching his breath. Before him stood Thanh. The strong breeze caught her silken-black hair and swept it across her face. She was dressed like a peasant in black pajamas and a conical straw hat. Even when dressed with such simplicity, her poise impressed him. Alexander had never seen anyone so stunning.

"Thank you for coming," she said in greeting, but without smiling. "This is my great uncle's house. He is a monk who lives alone."

A diminutive figure, his head shaved and dressed in the saffron robes of the Mahayana order, approached her side and nodded to Alexander.

"I came to visit Ho Thich before returning to France. My father sends his regards. He was unable to join us. Please, come in for tea." She pointed toward the house.

Alexander followed Thanh to the house. Inside, the hut was cool and dim, lit only by an open window with a view of the Gulf. Her uncle moved toward a small kerosene stove. The old gate guard remained outside. Thanh gestured for Alexander to sit at a small table under the window.

"I didn't know what to expect when the old man asked me to follow him," Alexander said.

"I told Ong Thieu that he should tell only you to follow him. Had anyone heard him ask you to meet me, too many explanations would be necessary."

The withered monk placed the tea on the table, sat down between them, and spoke to Thanh in an accent that Alexander could not understand.

"My uncle asks what brings you to this island," she said, pouring the tea through a tiny strainer into small porcelain cups. "I told him you were here with the Vietnamese Navy."

"How long has your uncle lived here?"

"Since 1954, after the great exodus from North Vietnam. Many people from the North settled in Cong Sa near Rach Gia. It is when my father came, too. Uncle Thich heard of other Buddhist monks on this island and came here to live. It is very peaceful."

"Yes, and the view is spectacular," said Alexander, glancing out the window. "Do you come here often?"

"When I was a small girl I would spend several weeks with Uncle Thich each summer. He gave me religious training, and I helped with the ginger harvest. Now I come perhaps once a year."

"Your uncle grows ginger?" Alexander asked, not knowing where to direct the conversation.

"Yes, and other crops, as do many of the monks who live on top the mountain," she said, raising her delicate chin toward the crest of the mountain. "After tea, if you wish, we will walk to the top."

"Yes, I would like to," responded Alexander.

The old monk spoke in a whisper to Thanh, then looked at Alexander.

"My uncle wishes me to tell you that he hopes the Navy's presence in the village will not bring the war to Hon Tre."

Alexander looked at the monk, whose hollow-eyed stare seemed to penetrate his thoughts. "Tell your uncle, and your father, that I share the same hope. We believe the war is coming to an end. Tell your uncle that the Americans wish to go home and leave your country in peace."

"Is that what the Americans wish? Some people say the Americans are the same as the French colonists."

Alexander recognized that this was not a translation from her uncle. "You are aware that we are removing our troops from Vietnam?"

"Yes."

"Then the action speaks for itself. We are not French. This is not 1950."

She spoke with the old monk for a few seconds. "My uncle asks why, if the war is coming to an end, there is so much bombing. The island shakes at night when your bombs fall."

Alexander nodded. At night he, too, felt vibrations from the distant bombing in the U Minh forest. "Those are the B-52's. The U Minh on the mainland is still controlled by the Vietcong. It is Nixon's plan to increase the strength of the Vietnamese military while maintaining maximum pressure on the VC as Americans withdraw. The bombing is to implement that strategy."

"Do you believe the war is coming to an end?" asked Thanh.

"Yes."

The old monk spoke to Thanh for several minutes, then he rose, nodded to Alexander, and stepped out the door.

"My uncle is very old and only wishes for the killing to end. He wonders who is doing the most harm to our people, the VC or the American bombs saving our people from the VC. Bombing for peace...it is difficult to understand, yes? But come," she said and rose, "enough politics. Shall we walk to the top?"

The old gate guard led the way back across the clearing and on to a trail that led into the foliage. The narrow path zigzagged up the mountain. In an hour they topped out onto the rounded crest. Below them they could see across the shallow Gulf to the mainland. The panorama was breathtaking, and the strong breeze filled their lungs with clean air. Thanh looked at Alexander and smiled for the first time.

"It is very beautiful, is it not?"

"Yes," he agreed. "It is beautiful. I have lived on the island seven months and did not know its beauty."

"The same is true of how most Americans look at my country."

Alexander smiled, bemused. Since meeting Thanh, their conversations always centered around the American presence, but it seemed only natural that the Vietnamese would be curious about the purpose of the Americans in Vietnam.

"Most Americans," he replied, "don't have an opportunity to look beyond the surface. But the surface, as it is with yourself, is often very beautiful."

With a slight blush, Thanh turned away and walked toward the far side of the crest. The mountaintop was randomly checker-boarded with cultivated plots and fruit orchards. Thanh explained to Alexander that most of the farmers here were Buddhist monks who lived in the small thatched houses near their cultivated crops, enjoying a simple, contemplative life. Here, high on the mountaintop they grew banana, cinnamon, apple, lime, jackfruit, yam, onion, ginger, tomatoes, and pomegranates. The granitic soil was obviously rich and productive.

"My father recently bought this plot," Thanh said, standing within the regular rows of an orchard. "It cost 470,000 piasters and will pay back in two years."

Alexander was somewhat surprised at her knowledge of her father's business. The role of women in Vietnam, he had been taught at counterinsurgency school, excluded them from tasks other than those related to the household or family. "How long has your father owned land on the mountain?"

"For as long as I can remember. As you can see, the farming here is very productive."

They spent an hour on top the mountain, walking among the orchards and cultivated plots. Alexander was astounded that such beauty and tranquility existed right on his own island. He wondered how much more about this country that Americans failed to understand, even though so much money and lives had been expended to defend it. Before descending, they shared tea with one of the monks. Looking out over the productive land with a view far across the Gulf to the mainland, Alexander understood why monks would be attracted to such a natural and spiritual environment so removed from the war. When they were returning, the trail dropped a few feet from one rocky ledge to another. Alexander turned and extended his hand to Thanh. Her palm felt soft and delicate in his.

Back at her uncle's house, Alexander was again impressed by the solitude and the striking view of the Gulf. The old monk had prepared fresh coconut juice mixed with lime and sugar, and had placed several boiled bananas in a serving dish. They ate and drank and discussed the crops. Alexander felt as if a door had opened to the warmth and hospitality of a people whom he had never known, yet for whose security he daily risked his life.

"I am happy you invited me to meet your uncle and to see the mountain," he told Thanh.

"I am happy you came," she replied.

"You said earlier today you would be returning to France. When will you leave?"

"In one week," Thanh answered.

"I would like to see you before you go."

"That is not possible. I have much to do before my departure. Now I must talk with Uncle Thich. Ong Thieu will take you back to the village. Thank you for coming."

Alexander rose and somewhat awkwardly extended his hand. Thanh took it in hers.

"*Au revoir*," she said.

"Good-bye." Reluctantly, Alexander let go of her hand, and turned and followed the old gate guard, who was already at the far side of the clearing.

The sun was setting when Alexander arrived back at the village. He spent the evening rocking slowly in the hammock, scratching Oink's ears, and staring at the bay until the gecko, whom he had named El Comandante, began clucking loudly, reminding him that it was time to turn off the lights.

# Chapter XIII

"Need some help, sir?"

Alexander looked over his shoulder. He had been trying to screen the unfinished wall of the advisor's hootch. Behind him he saw a tall, strapping boatswains mate third class balancing a duffle bag slung over his shoulder and sporting a boyish grin.

"Name's Brooks, sir," said the young newcomer. "I'm your new advisor."

Brooks was nineteen years old, a lumberjack raised in the forests of western Washington State. Alexander soon put his muscular frame and mechanical aptitude to use on the hootch. During the next two days they patched and completed the tin roof, screened the unfinished wall facing the bay, and cut a back door for an emergency exit to the trenches. Chain link fencing was secured around the foundation so that a satchel charge couldn't be tossed underneath. They lined the interior walls to shoulder height with sand bags and then paneled over the bags with plywood. They painted the outside of the hootch army green and hung a sign near the entrance that showed their island, shaped like a turtle, and that proclaimed "Hon Tre Junkies'.

After returning from patrol, Sanchez dropped by the renovations and nodded his approval. Alexander was by himself. He had sent Brooks to Rach Gia.

"Not bad for a three day patch-up," Sanchez said. "It's better than my place in the States."

"We finally got the new advisor day before yesterday," explained Alexander. "Brooks is his name, boatswains mate third class, and a first class carpenter."

"Thank goodness he's here," said Sanchez. He, like Alexander, was relieved that another advisor would share their patrol schedule. "Where is he?"

"I sent him on the 3:00 a.m. water taxi to pick up the mail in Rach Gia and to meet the NILOS. He told me he came to Vietnam for the adventure and excitement. I figured a three-hour boat ride with a load of seasick pigs would put this adventure in the proper perspective."

"Adventure and excitement? How about heat rash and diarrhea," replied Sanchez. "You taking him with you this afternoon?"

"Right. I think Brooks is going to be OK. Thank god we're off the port and starboard patrols. By the way, how was your patrol?"

"Not bad. The Army flew a couple of choppers over last night, but we had their freq's so no problems. Aside from that, it was seventy-two hours of rice, fish, and gooks."

"Adventure and excitement. Say hello to Tho."

With the hootch now in shape and a new advisor onboard to break up the patrols, Alexander appraised the outlook as nothing less than rosy. Coastal ops were a cakewalk compared to river patrols, and the food they pilfered from the fishermen was superb.

That afternoon Brooks returned from Rach Gia with the mail, full of stories about the water taxi. His unmasked enthusiasm was contagious. When the Dai Uy politely knocked on the advisors' door and in Vietnamese announced they were leaving on patrol, Alexander introduced his counterpart to Brooks. The Dai Uy merely nodded. He might treat an American lieutenant as an equal, but never a boatswains mate third class. Class distinctions in the third world were more guarded than in the wealthiest of nations.

Alexander methodically demonstrated the routines of a patrol to Brooks, emphasizing how to call in and direct artillery or Seawolf support. The key to a proper combat response, he explained, was in preparation and rehearsal.

At supper, rather than eat from the communal dishes prepared by the Vietnamese cook, Brooks opened a C-rat box. The Dai Uy winked at Alexander and nodded toward the roof of the junk where Brooks was eating by himself. Alexander, speaking in Vietnamese as he shared the dishes with the Vietnamese sailors, addressed the cook. "The big American prefers C-rats to your cooking."

The Vietnamese sailors broke into loud laughter. Cook jokes were universally appealing.

Later Brooks asked about toilet facilities, and Alexander pointed over the side of the boat. When the new advisor dropped his pants, the Vietnamese sailors began talking and pointing to his bare white butt. Embarrassed, Brooks pulled up his pants and climbed back on the cabin roof.

"What the hell were they looking at?" he asked angrily.

"Don't ask me."

"Do they stare and point at you, too?" asked Brooks.

"Nope."

"Why not?"

"Because I never crap on patrol. I can't stand an audience," replied Alexander, and jumped down to the deck to share hot tea with the Dai Uy, leaving Brooks to contemplate the cultural gap in all its glory.

Alexander encouraged Brooks to speak Vietnamese. The two most important tools an advisor had, he explained, were his radio and the ability to speak Vietnamese. "We seldom see any combat activity on coastal operations, although last month we were mortared from the Three Sisters," explained Alexander. "You're about as secure here as possible without being considered a REMF, a Rear Echelon Mother Fucker."

Just as he spoke an explosion sent shock waves through the still midday air. Every eye looked astern, where the smoke of an artillery burst wafted some three hundred yards behind the junks, thirty feet above the water.

"What in the hell?"

The distinct high-pitched howl from the burst could only be a 105 howitzer loaded with anti-personnel flashette rounds. As far as Alexander knew, the VC didn't have any such shells.

*Crumpf.* Another shell exploded, this one even closer to the junks.

"What the shit!" Alexander exclaimed.

The Dai Uy jumped to the helm, started the boat's motor, and yelled at the sailors to weigh anchor. A third round landed less than one hundred yards behind them. Alexander grabbed the PRC-25 radio and jumped from the roof to a bench on the deck below. The impact of his weight broke the wood and impaled his leg to the bench. Dragging the bench behind him, he shouted over the radio at Rach Gia. "Oscar Lima, this is Alpha Lima. Whoever's firing 105's, tell them to cease immediately! They're hitting too close to our boats!"

Rach Gia assured Alexander that no friendlies were firing in the area.

"Well, who the god damn hell is it?" he yelled. "Those are flashette rounds, and we're a half mile from the beach. It has to be our own 105's."

"Yes, sir. I've passed the information to the Army. It is not, I repeat not, friendly fire."

Alexander released the transceiver and muttered under his breath. "Shit for brains. Not friendly fire.

Jesus H. Christ!" He again pressed the transceiver and shouted in the radio. "You're right. It's sure as hell not friendly fire. Call the goddamn Army again and tell them to desist firing!"

When no further rounds exploded, Alexander spotted the Dai Uy in his cabin. He wondered why the Dai Uy was laughing. Alexander stared down at his foot, which was still stuck through the top of the bench.

"Brooks, get down here and help me out of this thing," commanded Alexander.

Brooks, who was grinning like a bear in a garbage pile, jumped to the deck and managed to extract Alexander's leg from the bench.

"Alex," the Dai Uy said, with a sparkle in his eye, "you jump off the roof too good."

"I was teaching Brooks how we fight the war," Alexander joked in Vietnamese. All the sailors and the Dai Uy broke into laughter again.

Later that afternoon Alexander called in a lengthy report to Rach Gia, describing the incident in detail. IV Corp headquarters conducted an investigation but failed to discover who had fired at the junks or if the junks were even the target.

# Chapter XIV

Alexander lay in the hammock, restless and contemplative. He had sent Brooks back on patrol with Sanchez. The evening meal had been cleaned up, and now only the insects made night sounds from the surrounding darkness. He tried reading a book but couldn't concentrate. Finally he put the book down, turned off the kerosene lantern, and stepped onto the porch. A thousand stars sprinkled the evening sky. With resolve in his step, he walked to the water taxi.

The old gate guard eyed Alexander suspiciously.

"I wish to see Ong Ngong," Alexander repeated.

"He is not here."

"Then please tell Co Thanh I wish to see her."

The green iron gate closed shut in Alexander's face. In a few minutes, the old man opened it again and, without comment, led Alexander to the house. In the dim foyer light stood Thanh.

"What are you doing here, Lieutenant?" she asked inquisitively. "My father is not at home."

"I really came to see you."

Thanh stared silently for a moment. "You should not be here."

"When I leave Vietnam, I can visit France. Perhaps we could meet again, if I knew where to contact you..."

Thanh blushed and replied, "That would be impossible."

"Would you care for breakfast?" asked Alexander, not wanting to terminate the conversation.

"My breakfast is ready now. You may join me, if you wish."

Alexander followed her to the dining room. She instructed a steward to prepare another serving. The light from an open window silhouetted her face, adding a backlit radiance to her delicate features. During the meal Alexander inquired about her background. He had surmised correctly that she had been educated in Paris. She told him she would soon be returning to her studies at the Sorbonne.

"And you, Lieutenant, when you leave Vietnam, where will you go?"

"To Texas, have you heard of it?"

"Certainly. Texas cowboys. The world knows of Texas. Did you volunteer to come to Vietnam?"

"Yes," he replied, "and I am glad I was sent here."

"Why?"

"It is an interesting experience, and as I learn about the people and your culture, I like them very much."

"And your politics?"

"Politics are for politicians. I am a soldier."

"In my country, they are the same."

After the meal coffee was served and they conversed about their childhoods. She told him that her brother was a captain in the ARVN. Her father had sent her to France to complete her education. As she spoke, gradually Thanh seemed to relax. Finally, though, she pushed her chair from the table.

"Lieutenant, I am happy you came. But now I must go. There are many things yet to do."

Alexander rose and blurted, "May I see you again, even if it's in France?"

Thanh hesitated, then took a small piece of paper from a desk, wrote down an address, and handed it to Alexander. "I live with relatives in Paris. Now, please, I must go. My father will be angry."

"Tell him I only came to report about Hon Tre. Thank you for another meal. It is my great hope to see you again."

"Yes," Thanh replied.

Alexander thought he detected concurrence in the manner that she spoke the single word. When he said goodbye, he held onto her hand for a few seconds, lingering. Too often in Vietnam, he thought, goodbyes were forever.


By mid-December coastal patrols settled into a predictable rhythm: three days on patrol, six days off. It was an easy schedule. Occasionally a VC sampan loaded with supplies of rice and *ba-xi-day* would be confiscated, or a few fishermen with false identification papers would be hauled to Rach Gia. Generally, however, one patrol was indistinguishable from another.

Shortly before Christmas Alexander took five days R&R to Sydney. After twenty-four hours of drinking and bar girls at Kings Cross, he returned to the R&R administrative center. For some reason he felt restless in the spotlessly clean and civilized city, so removed from his environment in Vietnam. Not caring for any more nightlife, he signed up for a three-day visit to the outback. Thousands of Aussies had agreed to take in American soldiers in Australia on R&R. Alexander's host family lived on a cattle and wheat ranch thirty miles from Holbrook in the western foothills of the Snowy Mountains. During the day he helped the father and young teenage sons work their Hereford cattle. In the late afternoon he'd take a swim in their pool before eating a wonderful dinner prepared by the mother and daughter. After dinner he and the father would drive thirty miles to the social club for a few beers and conversation.

Upon his return to An Thoi, Alexander stopped by Holloman's before checking in with headquarters and related the experience to his friend.

"Holloman, I'm not sure it really happened. To pick yourself up from this shit and parachute into security and a civilization filled with hospitable, warm, and generous people is a mind warp."

"Good Lord, Alex! In addition to paying you an

extra $55 dollars a month for hazardous duty, the U.S. government throws in a free round-trip ticket to Sydney for I & I — intercourse and intoxication — and you don't even sack it with one round-eye? And you're telling me it didn't even happen? Is this memory loss or brain decay?"

"Probably both. I just can't switch gears. Maybe we've been in-country too long."

"Myself, I'm just hanging on till DEROS," said Holloman. "This place is getting to me. I've even been thinking a lot about Brenda lately."

"Brenda, your old Pearl Harbor girl friend, the one you left your car with?"

"You know what distance does to the heart. She's been writing me forlorn love letters, and I'm beginning to think she's the one."

"I never thought you'd say that, Holloman. It *must* be getting to you. Did you hear that Sanchez re-upped last month for his fourth tour and asked me to help push his marriage papers through Bupers in Saigon? Maybe I could meet you there next month. You could give me the Cook's tour of Tu Do Street."

"Gook's tour is more like it. Hey, buddy, that sounds good to me. It'll get my mind off leaving this third-world dump. So Sanchez is still serious about marrying the slope? I figured with your cozy household arrangement for three, who needed marriage?"

"Don't throw stones at thatched houses, amigo. Besides I moved back to the advisor's hootch a month ago. Listen, I'll be in Saigon in two weeks. Where shall we meet?"

"Check in at the Continental Palace. I'll see you at there at the terrace bar. It's a great place for an early morning gin and tonic."

"Do you realize, Holloman, we're getting short? Four more months until DEROS. Doesn't seem like we've been here that long."

"Not if you like *nuoc mam*, gooks, and An Thoi's bullshit. It's been a wasted year for me. God, I'll be glad when it's over. Did you hear Jameson got a purple heart? He fell on a hot M-60 barrel and he wasn't even in a fire fight. He scalds his back, and gets medevac-ed to Japan. Sometimes I think I'll shoot myself in the leg. A crippled foot beats a crippled brain."

"Sounds like this place is getting to you."

"For me it's been a prison sentence."


Later in the afternoon Alexander met with Commander Schoen, who expressed his pleasure with Coastal Group 43's Market Time blockade efforts. The NILO reports on the reduction in the number of firefights were an indication that the VC had not recovered from the Cambodian incursion.

"In fact, Lieutenant, the Army has begun plans for a cordoning in the U Minh. We've pushed Charlie back into the forest enclaves, removed from the civilian population. Now we'll be shifting your coastal patrols south of the Cai Lon River. You'll be

159

working with Colonel Vann. Also we'll send you a civic action advisor. As Vietnamization progresses, we intend to increase pacification efforts."

"What sort of civic action, sir?" asked Alexander.

"Agricultural programs and medical assist for the villagers. As senior advisor you'll have control over the projects. Keep up the good work, and let me hear from you."

Back on Hon Tre Alexander met with the Dai Uy to discuss the move south to the Cai Lon. It came as no surprise to Alexander that the Dai Uy was aware of the pending change and anxious to start the new operations.

# Chapter XV

Less than a week after Alexander's return from R&R, a Huey 1-B helicopter circled over the base and, in a gust of blowing sand, landed on the beach in front of the Navy compound. A group of villagers gathered to watch. Alexander wondered what went on in their minds when confronted with such an instrument of the twentieth century. To confront an American helicopter which had dropped straight from the heavens in a rush of noise and a blast of wind had to be a startling experience for someone whose technology did not reach beyond hand-sawed beams. Nevertheless, the villagers reaction was one of curiosity rather than fear.

From out of the helicopter jumped A U.S. Navy non-commissioned officer, ducking to avoid the prop wash. Black as spades and sporting a wide smile, the NCO saluted Alexander sharply and proclaimed, "My name is Owens, sir. I'm with the civic action group. Did they tell you I was coming, sir?"

"Yes, welcome to Hon Tre, Owens. Bring your

duffle up to the hootch and let's hear what kind of civic action you have in mind."

Owens had grown up on a farm in the Mississippi Delta and had already spent two tours in Vietnam working with the navy's civic action farm program. On his first afternoon at Hon Tre Owens handed out Band-Aids to the island's kids, who proudly stuck them to their cheeks and foreheads. One look at the island's sway-backed pigs, and Owen started a jive step that the Vietnamese children began to mimic.

"Hey, tutti frutti, what that ham don't know is what his *backbone* is for," Owens exclaimed and pointed to one of the island's sway-back pigs. "They need roller skates on their gut to keep their *jewels* out of the coconut shells. What do you think, Loo-tenant? Ain't they the god-awfulest pigs you ever saw?"

"They do look pitiful, Owens," admitted Alexander. "Old Oink is about the best of the lot, and he isn't exactly a beauty. How long do you think it would take to breed a straight back?"

"Just let a couple of my big stud boars loose with these bitches for one month, and they'll have them ladies goose-stepping in single file with a grin as big as Baltimore. Hey man, these boars of mine are honky. Oink, my good man, you better stand aside. This ain't no place for the little league. *Love* and goodwill, here we come," Owens said with a broad grin. "Now," he added, "what about the chickens? I ain't seen no chicken operation on this place."

"Most of the villagers raise a few, but mainly they eat fish. Why do you ask?"

"What we need here is a chicken operation, Loo-tenant. Too much fish makes your eyes slant. I been trying to get Uncle Sam to invest in chickens for three years. All we need is a good financial advisor. Maybe this is the place to start, what do you say, sir? Chicken...it do go with rice."

Owens natural exuberance was uplifting, but after two days Alexander was happy to leave for patrol. When he returned Owens had left for the mainland, but his tracks were still evident. Under his direction the village children had manned a bucket brigade to refill the advisors' drinking water. Two more pups which Owens had named Flop and Bitch were residing with the advisors. Oink's new title was Guard Pig. When Owens departed on the early morning water taxi, half the kids in the village saw him off.

"So the Pied Piper was black," smiled Alexander to Brooks as he removed his boots. "When is he coming back?"

"He said he'd be here in two weeks with his two stud boars."

"Two stud boars. This place may never recover. I hope his boars can handle the boat ride without losing their lunch," mused Alexander.

After Brooks went on patrol that afternoon, Alexander showered under the canvas bag. Refreshed, he walked to the village and drank a few warm beers at the local bar. The moon was full. The evenings were less stifling than the days. Most nights Alexander could hear and distinctly feel the bombs hitting the U Minh, thirty miles away. Old Charlie puts up with some shit, thought Alexander, as he drifted into a quiet rest.

# Chapter XVI

"Looks like you beat me to the shrine. Howdy, my little Texas *amigo.*"

Alexander looked up at Holloman, who was standing in front of him with a wide smile under the Australian bush hat. Alexander was sitting at the Continental Palace terrace bar.

"Nice place you found here, Holloman," said Alexander. "This is the best array of pimps, prostitutes, dwarfs, and seedy-looking journalists I've ever seen. Somerset Maugham right here in Saigon."

"All in good taste. Have you ordered gin and tonics for us?"

Alexander looked at his watch. It was nine a.m.

"We have to maintain a constant vigilance against malaria, hear?" Holloman sat down at the table. "How is life on the tropical isle?"

"All is well," replied Alexander, "although we'll soon shift operations south to the Cai Lon River and to the coast adjacent to the U Minh. I may be getting too short for river ops." When the waiter brought their drinks, Alexander raised his glass to Holloman. "Here's to your health. How's life at An Thoi?"

"It's lovely, seen through a half-empty bottle of booze. Speaking of which," he raised his glass, "mud in your eye and down the hatch."

They sat in the bar all morning, drinking, discussing the trivialities of their advisory roles, and watching the fantastic parade of people passing by. The traffic on Tu Do Street was a mass of fumes, horns, trucks, cars, cyclos, and pushcarts. A political protest began nearby at the National Assembly.

"Come on," Holloman suggested after several drinks. "We've sat here long enough. Let's catch a cyclo to Ton Son Nhut".

"Ton Son Nhut? Why do we want to go there? Ton Son Nhut is nothing but airplanes and assholes," responded Alexander, who was feeling quite relaxed where he was.

"Trust me, my friend of little faith. I'll bet you fifty dollars I can beat you to Ton Son Nhut's east gate. Come on!" Holloman jumped up and ran into the street, where he waved down an empty cyclo.

Alexander threw enough money on the table to cover their bill and ran after Holloman. He also hailed a cyclo and jumped into the front seat, telling the driver in Vietnamese he'd pay an extra ten dollars if they got to Ton Son Nhut before Holloman. The cyclo driver hammered the throttle and began a mad chase through the traffic, straddling boulevards, squeezing between trucks and taxis, and taking turns so sharply he almost threw Alexander out into the street.

"I'll make it twenty dollars American," Alexander shouted. The driver gave the cyclo an extra push at an intersection of oncoming traffic in a blind man's bluff that miraculously worked. Alexander laughed and gripped his open seat at the front of the cyclo until they skidded to a halt in front of the east gate of the airport, a full thirty seconds ahead of Holloman.

He held out his hand to Holloman. "You know better than to race against me. Remember Crazy Horse Hill," Alexander said, reminding Holloman of a steep downhill pedicab chase in Hong Kong. On a hairpin turn Holloman's pedicab had tipped over, skinning the driver's leg and throwing Holloman into a fruit stand.

"Just checking your reflexes, partner. Let's hit the Vietnamese Air Force O-Club for lunch. You won the bet. You buy the drinks."

When they arrived at the O-club, a young Vietnamese *maître d* led them through an elegant chandelier-lit dining room, down a flight of stairs, along a passageway, and into a dimly-lit bar.

"It's plenty dark," Alexander commented. "You ever been here before?"

"Nope, but my Filipino girlfriend said this is our kind of joint. Speaking of which, you ever tried this shit?" Holloman took a cigarette from his front pocket.

"What is it?"

"Try it, you'll like it." Holloman lit up and handed the cigarette to Alexander. "Here, it'll make

167

you forget you're in Nam."

"Not me, Holloman. I'm pickling my brain with nothing but plain old alcohol."

As Alexander's eyes slowly became accustomed to the dark interior, he made out a dance floor and a long, elegantly carved bar at the far end. Tall-backed, cushioned booths lined the walls on either side. Other customers were in the room, but it was difficult to see them in the dim light. A stereo system played "Rolling on the River."

"What kind of place is this?"

"Relax, relax," said Holloman. He sucked contentedly on the joint, inhaling deeply.

After bringing their drinks, the waitress asked if Alexander would buy her a tea. She was petite with smooth skin and full lips, and was dressed in the traditional *ao dai*.

"Please," said Alexander in Vietnamese, "if you will join us. Also, your friend." He pointed to another waitress. "Will she join us?"

"*Mais oui.* We do not have many American visitors here, and few that speak our language."

The second girl sat down beside Holloman, who raised his drink and his eyebrows to Alexander. "Here we go again," he said as the second girl sat down beside him.

The next few hours were a blur. They continued to drink and buy tea for the girls. Holloman pulled down his girl's blouse and felt her small, firm tits. Alexander laughed and did likewise. At one point, a group of Vietnamese fighter pilots initiated a game of horse, which involved carrying the bar girls on their backs, shoving and pulling each other until everyone fell into a dog pile on the dance floor. Finally, drunk, bruised, and tired, Alexander decided to call it a day.

"Leave!" exclaimed Holloman, who was sprawled out on the dance floor. "You're bonkers, buddy. This has the makings of a three-day, red-white-and blue, all-American orgy, and you want me to leave? You're nuts!"

"Holloman, this isn't the place for horny gringos. Come on, we'll hit Tu Do Street where whoring is legitimate."

"They don't care. They love us. Come on, I'll buy you another drink."

Alexander paid out, tipped the bar girls, and waved goodbye to the Vietnamese pilots. Holloman reluctantly followed, complaining all the while about Alexander's piss poor judgment and misplaced morals. The sun was still high in the sky when they left the club.

"Goddamn, it's bright," said Holloman, blinking in the sun. "I thought it was past midnight. What time is it?"

"Time to get back to the Terrace Bar. Come on, let's ride together."

With arms around each other's shoulder, they saluted the gate guards, said, "Number one! Number one," and hailed a cyclo for the ride back downtown.

After bathing and changing into clean clothes, Alexander and Holloman left the Continental and walked down Tu Do Street toward the Saigon River, where they found a pleasant Vietnamese rooftop restaurant. They ate a splendid meal overlooking the boat traffic on the river. After dinner they rented a suite in a whorehouse and spent the rest of the evening in physical abandonment with their whores, emptying their minds of care, of responsibility, of military demeanor, of everything except the youthful, instinctive embrace of the moment.

The next morning as they walked back toward the Continental Hotel, the two friends ambled along, reviewing the evening's activities, laughing at certain recollections. Sunlight filtered through the majestic chestnut trees, creating speckled patterns of light and shade on the sidewalks. Alexander could understand why Saigon was called the Paris of the Orient.

Without warning a Military Police jeep stopped directly in front of them. Two heavy-set black MP's stepped out. "Where are your hats, gentlemen?" said one of them without saluting. "It's Army reg's to wear hats at all times when out of doors."

Holloman shook his head in amazement. "Hey, Bro, this is the Nam. What are you talking about, hats?"

"It's regulations, sir, no exceptions. You men will have to get off the streets or put on your hats."

Alexander couldn't believe his ear. "Listen," he said, stepping in front of Holloman. "We don't wear hats when we're in Saigon. Now, get out of our goddamn way." He grabbed Holloman by the arm, ready to make a run for it, but the MP's blocked their way. A crowd began to form. The jeep had blocked street traffic.

"You will have to come with me, sir. You're out of uniform and resisting the order of an MP."

Alexander caught Holloman's eye. "Shades of Guam," he muttered softly. Reaching into his pocket he pulled a handful of coins and Vietnamese currency and threw it at the feet of the MP's.

"Here's American money," he shouted in Vietnamese to the growing crowd. "Keep the monkey faces away from us!"

The crowd scrambled toward the money, engulfing the MP's.

"*Di di mau, amigo!*" Alexander hollered. They broke away from the crowd and ran in the opposite direction of the jeep. The two MP's shouted at them to stop, but the two advisors quickly disappeared down a narrow side street and dashed through the back door of an old mechanics shop. Excusing themselves to the startled occupants, they ran out the front to a busy street where they hailed a taxi and told the driver to take them to the Continental in a hurry.

"Where's your hat?" repeated Holloman. "Un-by-God-
believable!" He was still out of breath.

"I knew there was something about the boondocks I missed," responded Alexander. "Twenty-four hours around you and I'm already up to my neck in gendarmes."

# Chapter XVII

Back at Hon Tre, Sanchez thanked Alexander for helping push the marriage application through the military's maze of red tape. "By the way," he told Alexander, "Tho thinks she's pregnant."

"You're kidding? You're going to be a father. Congratulations, Sanchez. That's wonderful!" Alexander said and shook Sanchez' hand.

"Thank you, sir."

"Well, now we'll have to speed up the marriage...got to make this official. Hey, that's fabulous!"

"Thanks again."

"Sanchez, how does that make you feel about the U Minh operation?" Alexander asked.

"I'm ready for it. How about you?"

"I don't know. It's probably short-timer fever, but I get uneasy thinking about it. No doubt the Dai Uy is happy as a cockroach. Market Time is a tad tame for his blood."

"I think the Dai Uy likes war," Sanchez observed.

When Sanchez and Alexander walked outside the hootch, all the dogs and Oink rose and stretched. After saying goodnight to Sanchez, Alexander looked up into the clear night sky and recognized Orion, impassive and timeless as ever. It reminded him of the magnitude of his insignificance, which, he decided, was only suspended by the impact he made on those few lives he touched. My, but it was a beautiful evening.

On Coastal Group 43's first patrol up the Cai Lon, seven of the boats were mustered, even the old Kien Giang class junk with the high stem and aft cabin. In a sweep-line formation, the boats entered the wide mouth of the river, making a grand entry for all the fishing boats to see. The Dai Uy, Alexander decided, enjoyed a certain sense of drama.

After supper when they were anchored for the night in the middle of the muddy river, a small observation helicopter circled and was soon hovering immediately over the command junk. Alexander recognized the person peering out of the chopper's door. When the struts were still three feet above the deck, the Colonel jumped down to their boat.

Alexander was dressed in black pajamas, but nevertheless self-consciously saluted the Colonel. When Alexander introduced him, the Dai Uy, as always in uniform, smartly saluted the Colonel. This was the first time a U.S. Army Colonel had boarded a 43 junk, and the Dai Uy was obviously pleased. He issued a curt command to the sailors to prepare tea and set a stool on deck for the guest.

"Glad to have you in my AO again, Alexander," the Colonel said. "How is everything?"

"Fine, sir. Our group is glad to be off Market Time patrols. Searching fishing boats everyday is monotonous."

"Not to say ineffective," snapped the Colonel. "I want you to know that the U.S. Army and Navy will soon be conducting an operation that'll take us straight to the enemy. Harassing VC supply lines is a reasonable tactic but not nearly as effective as kicking them in the nuts. I have cleared the use of your junks with Commander Schoen."

The Colonel pulled out a topographic map and went on to explain the general objective of the upcoming operation. His intelligence group believed that three VC battalions operated from a large tunnel complex in the U Minh, virtually undetectable by aircraft, but expected soon to be pinpointed and destroyed. In support of the operation the 43 junks would spread out, covering each canal at the point where it intersected the coast. With the Colonel's and ARVN troops onshore and the junks offshore providing the blocking force, B-52's would serve as the striking force to eliminate the VC bunker complex.

"Our real problem is the ability of the VC to fade in and out of the forest area. It makes a head-to-head confrontation almost impossible," the Colonel continued.

"What do you mean 'fade'?" asked the Dai Uy,

who had been listening intently to his every word.

The Colonel looked sharply at the Dai Uy. The explanation had been directed to Alexander. He was surprised the Vietnamese had understood. "Disappear. We need to know where they are and where they escape to."

Before the meeting was concluded, the Dai Uy served the Colonel tea and a *consommé* with cucumbers dipped in *nuoc mam*. Alexander thought the snack delicious but could tell the Colonel was less than enthusiastic. In short order the observation helicopter had picked up the Colonel and whisked him away, its struts barely skimming the surface of the broad, flat river.

Alexander could sense the Dai Uy's excitement. "Alex, we can find VC. I know," he said in staccato English.

"What do you mean, Dai Uy?"

"VC fade. VC fade. But we know where. You wait, we find VC for Colonel."

"Good. Now, do you wish to hear some more 'Henry V'?"

"No, no. You read. I am thinking."


Their first patrol up the Cai Lon lasted four days but passed quickly. The junks patrolled up river as far as a large floating naval supply facility that had been turned over to the Vietnamese three months earlier. The Vietnamese Naval group had taken over operations from the U.S. Mobil Riverine Force and now had jurisdiction over the remaining inland waterways. The Vietnamese commander in charge of the floating base, who had a widespread reputation for graft, called in the Dai Uy to report to his headquarters. After he returned from the commander's stateroom, the Dai Uy was enraged, but never mentioned his conversation with the commander to Alexander.

When the junks returned to Hon Tre and entered the familiar bay, Alexander could see Brooks and Sanchez standing on the beach. They paddled out in a sampan to bring him ashore.

"Owens is back," reported Sanchez, as the sampan with Alexander in it pushed away from the boat. "And he brought his two boars with him."

"Good. Heaven knows, the pigs on this island need some better genes," replied Alexander. "There's nothing like a little civic action."

"Wait till you see the boars," said Brooks. "They are unreal."

A troupe of villagers, mostly children, were at the beach to meet the sampan. In their midst was Owens, teeth flashing and fingers snapping.

"Ho, Loo-tenant," he shouted, "so very happy to see you, sir. Top of the morning to you!" He gave Alexander a salute that resembled a high-five at a high school basketball game.

"Good to see you, too, Owens," said Alexander. "Brooks and Sanchez tell me you brought the boars."

"Yes, siree, sir. Took 'em two days to get over the

boat ride, but now they've totally recuperated and are standing duty. Me and the men," with a swoop of his arm he pointed at the ragamuffin group behind him, "already built their BOQ. We've co-signed every bitch pig in heat to a day of frolic like they ain't never seen before, ever."

"Owens, give me a chance to clean up and then come on up to the hootch and tell me about your plans." After four days on patrol Alexander wanted to shave and change clothes before being accosted by so much energy.

"I'll just follow you to the hootch now, if that's all right, sir. Brooks and I are roommates."

Alexander glanced at Brooks, who shrugged.

"Now, Loo-tenant, about the chickens. We'll need a place on base here, say two hundred feet by fifty..."

As they marched up the hill, leaving the children at the gate, Owens rattled on exuberantly about how the new generation of pigs and chickens would win over the hearts and minds of the villagers. After showering in the stall which Brooks had jury-rigged from two empty drums, Alexander played with the dogs and scratched the ears of Oink Johnson, who now weighed close to two hundred pounds. Finally, he let Owens escort him to the new pig pens.

"That, sir, is French Fry," Owens said, pointing to one of the huge pigs. "And over here," Owens pointed to the adjoining pen, "is Catfish. What do you think, Loo-tenant?"

The two pigs were huge pink-skinned Yorkshires. Each stood nearly three feet tall and weighed close to five hundred pounds. Their testicles were the size of cantaloupes. Alexander quickly checked the sturdiness of the boar's quarters. The pens had been constructed with new two-by-sixes, something Alexander had not been able to acquire, even for the advisors' hootch. The roof was made of shiny new tin.

"I never saw such huge pigs in my life, Owens. French Fry and Catfish. Are they friendly?"

"Just like big old butterballs, Loo-tenant. Here." He put his hand over the fence and began rubbing behind the ear of Catfish, who contentedly fell to his front knees and rolled over on his side, grunting with content.

"Now don't you try it, but for me, they ain't no animal more loving than one of these sweet things. You can own a dog, but man, you can *live* with a pig."

"I see," said Alexander. "The pens are well-built. Where did you get the lumber?"

"Nothing but the best for the boys," grinned Owens. "I've already put out the word to the people here on the island that whenever one of their sway-backed bitches is ready, to give old doc a call," Owens continued. "Then just stand aside and watch the fireworks. Man, you ain't never seen a corkscrew do its job till you see one of these dudes in action."

"Did you clear this with the village chief?" asked Alexander. He was afraid Owens would circumvent village politics, and the whole program might not work.

"Yes, sir. He's the one with the big square jaw, ain't he, who don't say nothing, just nods his head and let's his security man do the talking?"

"That's correct. Glad you cleared it with him. Owens, you may know more about civic action than I realized. What did the chief say?"

"He say...," and Owens rattled off some strange sounds meant to be Vietnamese. "Ho, ho, kidding aside, sir, he ain't got no problem, no problem. He gonna *love* the boys here. Shee-it, man, in no time at all we'll have this island covered with pink and black polka-dot pigs. Now, let's talk about the chickens."

"First, is there anything else to discuss about the pigs? Do you foresee any problems?"

"Loo-tenant, I was born on a pig farm, and raised on a pig farm. Hell, I may be part pig myself," Owens said, slapping himself on his large belly. "Everything is going to be all right, A-OK, Philadelphia. You don't need to worry about a thing."

"Come on, I'll buy you a *ba-muoi-ba* over ice," said Alexander, feeling better about the civic action program.

The Americans, dogged by Oink Johnson, walked down to the open-walled thatched structure that served as the bar. Dilapidated tables and chairs were scattered on the sand under coconut palms. Several locals were playing cards and talking in groups. On days the ice was brought from Rach Gia the bar attracted a crowd until the ice melted.

"Now, sir, about the chickens," said Owens

persistently.

"All right, Owens, what about the chickens?"

"You see, sir, chickens have to be raised by the book, none of this barnyard bullshit. You got to control their environment, see? So what we need is a big-ass, done-up-snuff chicken coop, say a hundred fifty by forty. Now, Loo-tenant, don't worry about the material. I'll handle the material. You just..."

"About the material, Owens," interrupted Alexander. "Where will you get it? That's a lot of lumber and tin and chicken wire."

"Now, captain..."

"It's *Loo*-tenant."

"No siree, from now on it's captain. You're like the captain of the ship, see? Rank don't mean shit when you the boss."

"Particularly when the boss is being led by the nose."

"Now come on, captain, we're in this together, ain't we? This is the Nam, come on."

Owens reached across the table and gave Alexander a dap handshake. Alexander couldn't help but laugh. He enjoyed Owens company and his enthusiasm, and was beginning to feel comfortable about his competency.

Owens explained he would have no problem procuring the materials and would get a Seabee group in Can Tho to erect the coop in two days. But he needed Alexander to negotiate for the land. He figured the coop should be built inside the base perimeter. A few thousand fryers might be too attractive a target for prospective chicken thieves. "We've got to have electricity for the incubators," Owens went on, "but I know where to get two portable diesel generators."

"Sounds like you have everything figured out, Owens. All I need to do is clear it with the Dai Uy, find you a spot for the coop, and you're in business."

"Well, captain, there is one other side to the equation. It's my blind side. It's...the money."

"The money?"

"Listen, captain. To get all this material, and the incubators, and the generators, and the feed, we can't go through Navy procurement. I mean, you don't exactly requisition a chicken factory from the Navy. They build ships."

"I thought this project was sponsored by the civic action program. What are you telling me, Owens?"

"Captain, I been down this road ten times before. The pigs are free. We don't even have to *rent* them. But chickens, now that's a different story. For a chicken operation, you have to go through USAID and ten thousand dead-end streets, and then you don't end up with nothing but excuses from people that ain't never seen the inside of a feather pillow. Unless, captain, unless you can help finance the operation. Then it'll slide smooth as goose grease, believe me."

Owens pulled a crumpled piece of paper from his pocket and showed it to Alexander. In hand-printed columns he had categorized the project and its cost. The bottom line was $2900.

"Let me get this straight," said Alexander. "You're asking me not only to clear this with the Dai Uy and find the land, but also to put up three thousand bucks to pay for this hair-brained chicken coop scheme?"

"It ain't *even* three thousand, boss. Believe me, it's the only way to get the project done before we pull out altogether. Anyway, this ain't no gift to the gooks. We gonna run a chicken *business*."

"I see. You intend to *sell* the chickens?"

"Captain, you're *too, too* fast for me."

The total scheme, painstakingly laid out by Owens, involved raising chickens on the Vietnamese Navy base, and then selling them in the market at Rach Gia. Chickens were in fact expensive, costing up to five dollars American for a good three pound fryer.


To Alexander's surprise, the Dai Uy was interested in the proposal. "How many chick-ens could it make?" he asked, after Alexander had laid out Owens' proposal.

Alexander was careful not to express his own doubts. "Owens says with three thousand chickens to start, after four months he could sell a thousand chickens a month."

The Dai Uy was impressed with the figures. "But Alex does not want to put down the money, yes?" asked the Dai Uy perceptively.

"Owens believes it would take three years to process the application for the funds and equipment through regular channels. Neither the Army nor the Navy has a chicken operation, so we would have to pursue it through non-military agencies. I am sure it would require a long time."

The Dai Uy stood up and walked to the window of his office. He looked out at the naval yard and back to Alexander. After thinking for a few moments, he replied to the proposal.

"We could not put the chick-ens on the base, Alex. Too much, too much payoff. People in the village can help, but not sailors. If people help, they must receive money. Alex, three thousand dollars...do you have that much? It is a fortune."

Alexander was dumbfounded. For the Dai Uy not only to listen to Owens' idea, but to ally himself wholeheartedly in the plan came as a complete surprise.

"You actually think the chicken operation would work?" Alexander asked, trying not to sound derisive.

"I think it is a good idea. We will discuss it more. You bring Owens to come talk tomorrow. Maybe we grow chick-ens." Before Alexander left, the Dai Uy asked, "Have you heard from the Colonel yet? When do we start the U Minh?"

"I don't know, Dai Uy. The B-52's have sure been hammering the U Minh, though." He referred to the tremors they felt every night from the distant bombing.

The next day Alexander and Owens met the Dai Uy and discussed in detail the plan to raise chickens. By the end of the discussion Alexander was completely convinced that Owens understood how to raise, feed, and care for a large chicken operation. Owens even had elaborate plans to barter a few chickens for discarded fish entrails, which could be mixed with the plucked feathers, ground into a mush, and heated to provide all the high-protein feed requirements.

"See, captain, we gonna convert fish guts and chicken feathers to four pound fryers to five dollar bills. Now ain't that the ticket? Shee-it, bro, this baby gonna fly."

Owen's colloquialisms fascinated the Dai Uy, who would repeat the American black jive talk with a Vietnamese pronunciation.

Not without misgivings, Alexander agreed to put up the money, with the understanding that it was strictly a loan that would be paid back from the proceeds of their first sales. A long discussion ensued between the Dai Uy and Owens about what to do with the profits. The Dai Uy insisted that half the profits be used to help the sailors and their families. Alexander looked at the Dai Uy and said, "Profits? There's an old American proverb. Don't count your chick-ens until the eggs hatch."

The Dai Uy held his hand to his mouth and broke into a muffled giggle. "An old Vietnamese proverb says," he replied, "be as an egg and profit from its strength."

184

"That must lose something in the translation, boss," interrupted Owens. "OK, gentlemen, give me three weeks to gather the goods, and then we'll launch the canoe, baby."

"Lonch the ka-noo?" repeated the Dai Uy.

"You know...start, kick off, commence, launch the canoe."

The Dai Uy nodded. "Lonch the ka-noo, yes."

# Chapter XVIII

To avoid visual detection the junks pulled out of Hon Tre after dark and headed northwest towards the Three Sisters. Halfway to the mainland they turned and pointed south toward the U Minh. Four of the junks towed captured sampans. Alexander gazed at the coastline and could detect tall treetops silhouetted against the thin flat horizon. The sea was choppy, causing the junks to roll and pitch. When their prows sliced into the waves, the wind spewed water across the decks.

Alexander had asked Sanchez to accompany him on this patrol, two advisors being more effective when the junks scattered out. There was only one Starlight scope, but they both carried PRC-25 radios. In the cool of dawn the Dai Uy and Alexander examined their maps and noted their progression down the coast. The junks were to be stationed close to shore near the mouths of small canals. The Colonel had assigned them a patrol area extending more than eight miles, which stretched thin their firepower. Alexander knew that two other coastal groups were also involved in the operation and assumed they were stationed further south down the Ca Mau peninsula. The cordon seemed awfully loose to pen an elusive and, as yet, undetected adversary.

The first day their boats conducted routine Market Time patrols. The Dai Uy sent sailors onboard the fishing boats to examine their interior and bilges for weapon caches. He also personally interrogated the fishermen for information about any VC they may have seen. The responses were invariably negative or noncommittal. It was clear that a large VC force could not survive or operate without the assistance of a significant number of collaborators, some of whom were undoubtedly boat people. Identifying VC sympathizers, however, was one of the challenges in this frontless war.

Prior to the patrol Alexander had received new KAK codes from the NILOS and was relieved that, even this far south, he had clear radio communications with Rach Gia. He carefully scanned the skies for helicopter activity that would signal the start of the impending operation, but he could see nothing out of the ordinary.

It was late in the afternoon when a large fishing boat was pulled over. The Dai Uy quizzed the owner, an old toothless fisherman, wrinkled and dark-skinned as a prune. The man nodded several times and pointed back toward the shore. The Dai Uy brought the old man onboard the naval junk and led him to his cabin. Alexander joined them but could not understand their low-voiced conversation because of the old man's dialect. "What did he say?" he asked, after the Dai Uy allowed the old man to return to his boat.

"He say Vietcong have checkpoint twenty minutes up the canal where he lives. He does not like the Vietcong. They take too much rice, too many fish," the Dai Uy responded. "Maybe tonight we go look."

Alexander stared at the Dai Uy's composed face. He had observed this expression before and knew what it meant. He climbed back to the cabin roof and began cleaning his M-16 rifle and M-79 grenade launcher.

As the last coral-tipped thunderheads faded to pale gray, the junks weighed anchor and proceeded in single file toward the coast. When darkness fell, through the Starlight scope Alexander could clearly see the outline of tall trees close ashore. Their black silhouettes were ominous, concealing no telling what in the forest of darkness, the U Minh. When he spotted a canal, which appeared as a black breach in the silver line of beach, he would point it out to the Dai Uy, who then had one of the sailors check the depth of the water with a weighted line. After circling the location on his map, the Dai Uy directed one of their junks to anchor near the mouth of the canal. It took almost two hours to station the boats in front of the canals. Because they were spread so far apart, the junks would not be able to support each other in a firefight.

The moon rose in the sky, a thin cusp that reflected too little light for any visual detection of activities. The sailors would have to rely on sound to detect coastal traffic coming or going from the canals.

The Dai Uy guided his junk back up the line until it was alongside Sanchez's junk, which was commanded by a young buck-tooth ensign whom the Dai Uy trusted. The young Vietnamese officer and Sanchez stepped aboard the Dai Uy's boat.

"Sure dark, isn't it?" said Alexander in a whisper to Sanchez.

"Yes," replied Sanchez. "Is that break in the beach a canal?"

"Right. These canals don't go very far inland. The forest is close to the beach. Here, take a look through the scope."

The shallow Gulf, the salty smell of the sea, and the rhythmic slapping of waves against the wooden hulls created an anomalous tranquility. Alexander and Sanchez whispered together until close to eleven o'clock, when the Dai Uy called for Alexander. Alexander could barely see the Dai Uy in the dark interior of the tiny cabin.

"Alex, we are here." The Dai Uy pointed to a spot on his map, which he was examining with a flashlight. Alexander had brought his own map and concurred.

"The old fisherman tell me the Vietcong stay here." The Dai Uy's finger traced the line of a canal on his map. The canal ran inland approximately one kilometer then, at a ninety degree bend, ran parallel to the coast. "He say they leave every morning down this way," pointing south down the canal that ran parallel to the coast. "Tonight we go in sampan and wait until they come. Maybe we can see where they go. What do you think?" He looked up at Alexander.

"You think we can follow them?"

"No," responded the Dai Uy. "But they come to the same place every morning to collect food. We can see where they go, where they fade. You understand?"

Alexander understood, but tracking the Vietcong seemed like an impossible task. Their base camp would be hidden in the forest or in any of the hamlets scattered close to the coast. Knowing there was no way to dissuade the Dai Uy, he considered staying behind, but he knew that the one refusal would create a chasm in their relationship that might never be bridged. Whoever named the Americans 'advisors,' he thought, used the wrong word. Artillery support, Seawolf support, and logistic support was what the Vietnamese wanted, but advice...never.

Alexander laid out the Dai Uy's plans to Sanchez. "What do you think?"

"It's risky. If the VC see you, you're on your own. You'll be too far away for help."

"We'll stay hidden and watch where they go. The Dai Uy is no fool."

Sanchez did not respond.

"Listen, Sanchez, I'm going along. I'll take my radio and will let you know where we are by clicking off the location like this." Alexander showed Sanchez a simple code that would relay their position. "I'll check in every two hours on the hour. The Dai Uy says we won't return until daylight. By then maybe we'll know where the VC fade."

Sanchez shook his head at the word 'fade,' which had become a joke between them.

Alexander put on his flak jacket and laced his boots. He left his M-16 at the junk but took the Starlight scope and the M-79 grenade launcher and a dozen rounds.

After the moon had completely set, the Dai Uy and two sailors stepped into the sampan alongside the junk. Alexander noticed for the first time the Dai Uy was also wearing black pajamas.

"Good luck," Sanchez whispered as the sampan pushed off from the boat. "And be careful."

The sailors paddled the sampan quickly toward shore. The tide was at full ebb. The pounding surf muffled any other sounds except for the waves lapping the shore. Within a few feet of the beach they could see the canal mouth, a short dark break less than twenty feed wide in the forest's silhouette. Alexander extended his paddle into the water and touched bottom.

When they entered the canal, the dark undergrowth seemed to swallow their sampan. As they moved cautiously down the canal, the sound of the surf faded behind them. Closer to the Gulf the canal's banks were thick with a growth of stunted trees and nipa palms, but farther inland the canal vanished into the forest, the tall trees forming a canopy of ink-black shadow.

They paddled silently, pausing at regular intervals to listen for coughing. The silence was eerie and ubiquitous. Alexander kept his eyes glued to the Starlight scope, searching for movement ahead or for deflected lights from the banks. The canal became a constricted tunnel, eclipsed by the forest. When within two hundred yards of the ninety-degree bend, they stopped the sampan on the south bank and grabbed hold of overhanging limbs.

The Dai Uy pulled Alexander's ear next to his lips. "I go look. You stay here." He took the scope, grabbed the thick roots extending into the water, pulled himself up the bank, and in a few seconds disappeared into the black jungle.

Alexander looked at the luminescent hands of his wrist watch. It was two o'clock. He turned on his PRC-25 and keyed the transceiver twice. Sanchez's acknowledgement was immediate and reassuring. The minutes dragged by with agonizing slowness. He didn't hear the Dai Uy when his small frame suddenly appeared on the bank and dropped silently into the small boat.

"Alex, you come with me," whispered the Dai Uy in his ear. "I find good place to hide. We watch VC. I send sampan back to junks. They pick us up tomorrow morning."

He gave a few whispered orders to the two sailors and scrambled back up the bank. Alexander handed his M-79 and radio to the Dai Uy and scrambled after him. Standing in the muddy ooze, which gave off a stench of organic decay, Alexander felt terribly out of place. With a boat deck under his feet he was always at ease, but the grip of *terra firma* felt alien.

Alexander followed the Dai Uy painstakingly through the dense foliage, directly away from the canal. The air was tepid. Not the slightest breeze stirred the vegetation. Mosquitoes swarmed around his body and face in thick clouds. Soon Alexander broke into a full sweat. Where his clothing stuck to his body, the mosquitoes attached themselves in clusters, their bites penetrating the thin, damp fabric. His legs and knees became caked with mud, and vines and sharp limbs scratched his hands and face.

They reduced the risk of booby traps by avoiding trails, which made their progress tedious. After struggling through the undergrowth for close to an hour, they reached a narrow stream. Raising the scope, the Dai Uy scanned upstream and then cautiously crawled into the water. Slinging his M-79 over his shoulder, Alexander followed. Submerged up to his chin in the lukewarm water, he felt more secure.

They pulled themselves forward in the shallow stream hand over hand, dragging their feet along the soft bottom. Both wore conical peasant hats and moved ponderously up the stream like straw turtles swimming in pitch. The underbrush completely engulfed them. Finally they reached the bank of the canal again, having intersected it beyond the ninety-degree bend. A few acres of forest had been cleared on the opposite side of the canal. Through the scope Alexander could see a bamboo and thatched hut beside a well-traveled path.

The Dai Uy tapped him on the shoulder, then crawled out of the water where the foliage completely encased the small stream. Not far from the stream, they stopped.

The Dai Uy whispered, "We stay here. Can watch VC."

Alexander nodded, his heart pounding from the exertion. The darkness was thick, liquid, opaque. No breeze stirred. Mosquitoes descended in squadrons. The hands on his watch showed four thirty. Shit. He turned on the radio, keyed the transceiver twice, and immediately received Sanchez' response.

They had probably crawled less than half a mile, yet he was physically and mentally exhausted. Methodically he began removing leeches, turning them counterclockwise before pulling.

In the tenebrous gloom his other senses quickly overrode the dominance of vision. The night sounds, at first a muffled undercurrent, became amplified and distinct. By slowly turning his head he could pinpoint the source of an insect's movement. He felt the wet earth and smooth roots against his skin. Here, in the dense U Minh, dangerously close to an enemy he had never seen, physically exhausted, Alexander felt intensely alive. Past and future, birth and death merged into one. For the first time he experienced a direct, spontaneous perception of the present. His year in Vietnam became a spiritual progression, culminating now and here, where he intensely felt the flux and web of time. Alexander's thoughts were interrupted when the Dai Uy touched his knee. "They come."

The faint murmur of a small engine intruded into the stillness. Its two-cycle motor gradually increased in loudness. He clutched his M-79 and squinted, willing his vision to proclaim dominance over the darkness.

For a moment he thought they had been discovered. The motor grew louder and louder, but then passed them, a Doppler effect in slow motion. Within minutes Alexander heard muted voices from down the canal. The Dai Uy wriggled forward and Alexander followed. At the edge of the canal, the foliage thinned. The Dai Uy raised the Starlight scope, looked across at the clearing, then handed it to Alexander.

Alexander saw four Vietcong squatting beside the hut. He could see them so clearly, it seemed as though he could reach out and touch them. One inhaled on a cigarette and the glow lit up his pock-marked face, as if highlighted by a campfire. Alexander was mesmerized by the nearness of the four Vietcong. At last he had seen the face of the enemy.

Finally he put down the scope and exhaled. The night's shadows were fading into the soft, semi-light of dawn. He and the Dai Uy inched farther back from the bank and lay motionless on the damp ground, waiting and watching.

With the coming of daylight, boat traffic along the canal commenced, gradually becoming a steady procession as the fishermen headed to sea. The sampans and fishing vessels lined up by the hut where the people handed over quantities of fish, rice, dried shrimp, and vegetables to the VC. No doubt this collection point had operated for many months. Every boat entering or leaving the Gulf from this quadrant had to pass by and offer contributions. Simple geography dictated its location, a natural choke point for canal traffic to and from the Gulf. Alexander made a mental note to examine his topo map to identify additional collection points.

By eight o'clock no more fishing traffic passed the collection point. The VC dug in their large cache of food and began to prepare breakfast. The aroma from the cooking caused Alexander's stomach to growl. After eating and cleaning up, the four VC loaded the mornings' collection and climbed into their boat. The man in the stern, the one with the face marred by small pox, appeared to be the leader. He started the Briggs and Stratton motor and within a few seconds, the VC boat passed Alexander and the Dai Uy.

From their hiding place Alexander saw a set of faded red eyes, the eyes of the dragon, painted on the boat's bow over an unusual yellow-and-gold background.

The Dai Uy waited quietly until the sound of the motor could no longer be heard, and then stood up and stretched. "What do you think, Alex? We find VC, yes?"

"For sure. They would have been easy to kill."

"I know, but we go for bigger catch," said the Dai Uy.

"What do you mean?"

"We will follow them," the Dai Uy replied nonchalantly. "Now I am hungry. Mosquitoes already eat breakfast."

Alexander felt his whelp-covered face. The only good thing about the swamp mosquitoes was the short duration of their sting. He was also hungry and mentally fatigued.

The Dai Uy picked up the radio, dialed the junks' channel, and started jabbering over the transceiver. Within an hour four sampans loaded with sailors and weapons rounded the bend and stopped at the hut. One of the boats picked up Alexander and the Dai Uy from the opposite bank.

Alexander was happy to see Sanchez. He was anxious to discuss the Dai Uy's idea of following the VC.

After eating a quick breakfast, the Dai Uy and the young buck-toothed ensign huddled in the shade of the hut. He had given orders for the others to spread out but had warned them to avoid moving around the clearing in case of booby traps.

Sanchez handed Alexander some salve to rub on his hands and face, and together they examined the topo map and located the thin blue line that represented the adjacent canal. After the right-angle bend, it ran south, parallel to the coast. There was no habitation on the swampy terrain close to the shore, but next to the dense forest, on the inland side, the map indicated several hamlets sprinkled along the canal.

"How does the Dai Uy expect to follow the VC?" asked Sanchez.

"There's only one place for them to go." Alexander pointed to the canal. "I told the Dai Uy that trying to find them now doesn't make sense."

"The fishermen who return this evening will pass the word that our sailors were here," said Sanchez.

"That's the problem. Sanchez, crazy as the goddamn thing sounds, I'll go on with the Dai Uy. What does he think we'll do when we find the VC...say hello and introduce ourselves? You return to the junks so we can maintain radio contact. I'll relay our location as we move down the canal. If the shit hits the fan, call the Seawolves ASAP. This is making me nervous."

"You want me to go with the Dai Uy?" asked Sanchez.

Alexander appreciated the offer and fully understood its measure. "Thanks, but no thanks, Sanchez. I've come this far with the little fucker..."

The Dai Uy walked up to the advisors, nodded to Sanchez, and unrolled his map. All except one sampan would proceed down the canal. The one would carry Sanchez and two sailors back to the command junk. They would search every hamlet along the canal for about twelve kilometers until reaching a larger canal. At that juncture the larger canal dissected their coastal canal and emptied into the Gulf. They would meet the junks off the mouth of this second canal. Alexander confirmed that he had communications with Rach Gia.

As they loaded into the sampan, Sanchez looked at Alexander. "Keep her in the road."

Alexander smiled and flashed a peace symbol.

The line of sampans moved out in close formation. The canal banks were impenetrable with thick vegetation. Occasionally they passed open spaces, once old fields, now abandoned and overgrown. At the first hamlet the lead sampan pulled to the opposite bank and the sailors, weapons ready, scrambled ashore and spread out in a line of support fire. The other two sampans tied up near the hamlet.

The hamlet looked like any other in Kieng Giang Province. Most of the bamboo-frame thatched houses had open porches extending over the canal, and narrow wooden berths for the sampans and small fishing boats that plied the coastal waters. In all, there were less than a dozen structures.

The villagers were mainly old women and small children. They looked impassively but suspiciously at the sailors. Dogs barked and a few chickens scattered as the Dai Uy methodically searched each house. The villagers' indifference was expected, but Alexander was puzzled by the Vietnamese children's lack of curiosity. They showed no interest in the American, not even begging for souvenirs.

The search uncovered nothing. When back in the

sampans, the Dai Uy grinned at Alexander. "I think they are VC," he said in English.

"Really, why?" asked Alexander.

"I do not know how to explain. You call Sanchez and tell him where we are."

They continued down the canal, searching the tiny hamlets, which were inaccessible except by the canal or by helicopter. At noon the boats stopped and tied up in the deep shade of low, overhanging branches. After a meal of cold rice and fish, all the Vietnamese sailors except for two guards slumped over their weapons and took their regular midday nap, which was religiously observed no matter what the circumstances.

Alexander, exhausted from the previous night, fell into a heavy sleep. When he awoke he felt muddle-headed and listless. He took off his shirt and lowered himself into the canal. Most of the other Vietnamese were now awake, too. One or two others jumped in the canal. The Dai Uy was studying his map again.

"Alex, where you think VC go?" he asked.

Alexander, who was submerged to his shoulders in the muddy, leech-infested water, shook his head. "They must have come down this canal. Perhaps they went up a stream." Alexander was referring to small streams that the canal intersected.

"Perhaps, but all the streams are too small, except maybe this one." The Dai Uy pointed to his topo map, and was speaking more to himself than to Alexander.

"I am sure the villagers know, but they will not tell us," said Alexander.

Back in the sampan, refreshed and alert, he pulled out his own map. At the confluence of the two canals close to where they would meet the junks, one hamlet, Ap Lon, appeared larger than the others. Further south the sector was sparsely inhabited and was an ideal location for the VC.

The afternoon was growing late. The Dai Uy's hopes for locating the VC began to wane. Alexander, however, was relieved. Taking a small group of untrained sailors this far from any effective air or artillery support was a job for the SEALS. It made him uneasy.

As they approached the last village, Alexander noted the houses were spread out on both banks of the canal. The larger canal ran perpendicular to their canal and into the Gulf. A good place for a collection post, he thought. Once again, the support team offloaded on the opposite bank, and the other two sampans offloaded at the hamlet. Once again they found only old women chewing betel nut and a few very young children, naked from the waist down, who stared silently at the sailors as they searched the first houses.

The sun's ray slanted across the rooftops, casting long shadows toward the canal. Alexander's stamina was wearing thin. His head throbbed and his muscles were stiff. He called Sanchez on the radio and told him they should be back in time for chop-chop.

When the Dai Uy began searching the houses,

Alexander held back. A movement from across the canal caught his attention. His gaze fixed on one of the boats tied to a short pier at the confluence of both canals. He recognized the fiery red eyes of the dragon against the unusual yellow-and-gold background on its bow. Trying not to sound alarmed, he softly called the Dai Uy.

The Dai Uy moved toward Alexander, who squatted on his haunches like a Vietnamese peasant, intentionally reducing his mass. Carefully, Alexander cocked the M-79 and stared directly at the Dai Uy, trying to let him know with his expression that something was wrong.

The Dai Uy looked across the canal at the sampan with the dragon eyes. Before Alexander could shout a warning, a sudden burst from an AK-47 shot from the house on the opposite bank, less than forty feet away. As if in slow motion, the Dai Uy's head exploded with the impact of a bullet, like a ripe melon dropped on pavement. Shocked and confused, Alexander stared open-mouthed at the Dai Uy's body. At the same time he was engulfed in a fiery maelstrom. He threw himself to the ground, firing his M-79 grenade launcher at the opposite bank. Bullets whirred inches above his head. He wasn't sure where they came from. Lying face down in the muddy earth, he searched the area for cover. God damn, he thought, ambushed!

He shouted in the radio to Sanchez, "We're hit! We're hit!" and fired two more rounds toward the opposite bank. The crack and *burrp* of automatic weapons split the air. His eyes landed on the lifeless body of the Dai Uy. An ashen grey pall of death already muted the color of his skin. Bodies began to fall around him. No fucking cover, goddamn it. I've got to get out of here.

The closest cover of any kind was a small group of trees behind him. Without raising his head, he fired two more rounds in quick succession and crawled backwards toward the trees. Too afraid to look up, he kept his cheek pressed to the mud. No bullets spattered around him. He heard firing where the first sampan had unloaded and shot two more grenades in the general direction. He checked his ammo. He had only three more rounds.

Behind him was a flat, abandoned field. A quarter mile away nipa palms marked the edge of the swamp. The ambush had been so well executed there was no doubt in Alexander's mind that the VC had known of their approach. He looked again at the Dai Uy's body. This can't be, he told himself. He looked around again. There was no place to run and no place to hide. He saw his radio lying on the ground. It was his best weapon, but the Seawolves were too far away to help. His heart pounding, his thoughts incoherent, he kept repeating to himself, over and over "Ambushed and no fucking cover, no fucking cover..."

The firing died to a few shots far across the canal. He heard a shout and watched as seven VC dressed in black pajamas and carrying AK-47's stood up and started moving toward their location. His options flashed through his mind. Do I shoot my last rounds and break for the swamp? Or should I go for the canal? Even if he could kill two or three of the VC, he knew his chances for escape were next to nil. Too far from the goddamn cover. Better to lie still. Any movement would give away his location. The coming darkness might provide the cover he desperately prayed for. Maybe the VC would leave. Maybe they were as frightened as he was.

Several dead sailors lay on the ground. The VC began rifling through their clothing, removing watches and boots, and then methodically shot each sailor in the head. When the bullets hit their heads, they bounced forward like basketballs. More VC arrived, jabbering loudly. Two of them walked over to the Dai Uy. Alexander shut his eyes, feigning death, and praying to God that he would not be discovered. No fucking cover, goddamn it, he kept saying to himself.

He heard a shout in Vietnamese. "There is one more. Here, take the radio. Hurry, the helicopters will arrive soon."

Alexander could hear footsteps rushing toward him and heard the metallic click of a bullet thrown into a rifle chamber. He opened his eyes and looked at the startled face of the VC who was about to blow his brains out.

"*Ban toi*," growled Alexander.

The VC stepped back out of Alexander's reach and shouted, "American, alive!" He kept his rifle pointed at Alexander's head.

Another VC approached. Alexander remained motionless, like a treed animal, frozen by the certainty that he was going to die. He recognized the pock-marked face from the early morning vigil.

"Shoot him, hurry, and let's go," one of them said.

"No," replied the pock-marked one. "We capture him." Then he walked to Alexander, raised his rifle, and smashed the butt of it into Alexander's jaw, knocking him unconscious.

# Chapter XIX

Alexander came to slowly, his mind muddled and disarranged. He felt as if his chest had been split by an axe. His arms were tied so far behind his back both elbows touched. Semi-conscious, he was aware of movement and the sound of a motor. They were in a sampan traveling rapidly through dense foliage in the forest. He couldn't have been unconscious for too long, as darkness had not completely fallen. His boots had been removed. He spat blood and tried to clear his thoughts. Captured! Oh God, why didn't I run for it? Why didn't I even try? Afraid and dazed by the pain, he slumped forward.

Slowly his thoughts began to clear. He'd been captured, but was alive. Captured, but alive. One thought came to mind: the first rule from SERE training was to escape at the earliest opportunity. The longer in captivity, the smaller the odds of escape. He wondered what would happen to a POW this far from Hanoi. He had heard rumors of other Americans being held in the U Minh. A prisoner this far in the South was no bargaining chip. Still, he was alive.

He looked up and attempted to gain his bearings, but the VC sitting behind him jerked at his bindings and shoved his foot into Alexander's back. He almost lost consciousness from the excruciating pain that shot through his back and chest. His arms felt detached from their sockets. Gasping for breath, he hunched forward and lay still, trying to alleviate the pain and concentrate on regaining some measure of mental control. How could he possibly escape? No matter what happens, he decided, I've got to try.

He considered overturning the sampan, but bound as he was, and surrounded by VC, escape now was impossible. Got to play the probabilities, he thought, stick to the odds, and wait for an opportunity. Don't make a stupid attempt.

Swallowed by the forest and absorbed by the darkness, Alexander could hear a sampan in front of them and another behind them. The stream along which they traveled was less than ten feet wide but deep enough for sampan traffic. This had to be the stream that ran to the village where they were ambushed. His thoughts lingered on the Dai Uy, whose death was still unconceivable. The futility, the utter hopelessness of escape kept occupying his thoughts. Where could they be taking me? What will they do with me?

For an hour the sampans crept slowly up the narrow waterway, the dark jungle absorbing any sign or sound of their passing. Finally the sampans slowed to a near halt. Alexander heard voices, and a flashlight shone down from a tree. His boat pulled to the bank and its motor stopped. He saw several small beams of light and heard voices. The VC behind him pulled his bindings and pushed him forward. Another grabbed his hair and dragged him to shore. He fell down on his side. The pain in his chest and shoulders was unbearable. A flashlight shone in his face.

"Here's the monkey face," someone said and kicked him in the groin. Unable to think about anything but the pain, he was oblivious to what was being said but was aware of someone grabbing his arms and pulling him to his feet. Dizzy and confused, he was led through the jungle. For nearly two hours they marched along a trail. Each time he stumbled someone would wrench his arms or yank his hair. His feet became tender and raw. He lost all feeling in his arms. His jaw was either broken or dislocated. Nevertheless, he willed his body to move forward, willed his tender feet to take a step, certain that if he collapsed he would be executed.

The trail widened into a narrow opening clear of undergrowth, but concealed by a canopy of huge trees overhead. He saw several bunkers tucked around the perimeter. A line of men carried long, wooden crates along a trail surfaced with strips of bamboo. Alexander's captors pushed him through an entrance guarded by two vicious dogs, and down a narrow, earthen stairway which led to a low tunnel. He was jostled along a narrow corridor that led into a dimly lit, low-ceilinged antechamber. Three tunnels led into the room, each one guarded by a VC holding an AK-47. Alexander was pushed down another narrow passageway less than four feet high and sparsely lit by flickering lanterns, which cast eerie shadows against the earthen walls. The tunnel, which twisted and turned in a confusing maze, was often ankle-deep in water. Occasionally they passed rooms stacked with wooden cartons. One large room with wounded soldiers on bamboo beds was obviously a field hospital.

After stumbling through the tunnel system for a long distance, they entered a room containing a low, narrow table and several stools. Two kerosene lanterns cast a sickly, flickering light. Alexander was thrown to this knees, his back shoved against the dirt wall. He could smell the fecund earth.

Scene by scene, he tried to review the sequence of events that had led him to this place, but dazed, bewildered, and exhausted, it was like leafing through a photo album in jerks and snatches. He could make no sense of it, could not grasp its reality. There was nothing he could do but wait, terrified and alone.

Alexander heard voices. Several Vietcong straightened upright as they entered the room, filed to the table, and sat down. Alexander choked back a cry. He recognized one of the faces. It was Thanh. Her eyes, which once reflected mystery and beauty, looked at him coldly, showing neither recognition nor expression.

Alexander was surprised that he was not immediately acknowledged by the VC, but a slight, older Vietnamese commanded the others' attention. They debated among themselves for several minutes. Alexander understood enough Vietnamese to determine that the floating Navy complex in the Cua Lon river near Nam Can had been targeted for a major sapper attack. Fearing they might discover he spoke enough Vietnamese to follow the conversation, he shut his eyes, feigning unconsciousness.

A kick to his rib cage made him gasp and fall over on his side. He was pulled up by his bindings and shoved toward the table. Across the narrow table sat the VC commander, and next to him sat Thanh.

"What is your name, rank, and serial number?" she asked officiously in her lilting French-English accent.

Confused and shocked, Alexander could only stare at Thanh. Once again, someone jerked his bindings and slammed his forehead down onto the table.

"J. D. Alexander. Lieutenant. U.S. Navy. 736486."

"What is your billet?"

Still stunned by Thanh's presence, he couldn't answer.

"Answer the question."

His elbows were pushed upward, and the pain shot through his shoulder sockets. He thought his chest would rip apart. "Advisor," he gasped. He did not intend to betray the code of conduct, but the pain was excruciating, and Thanh already knew he was an advisor.

"What is your unit?"

He remained silent until the bindings around his elbows were grabbed and slowly raised, causing him to scream in anguish.

"Coastal Group 43." His breath came in short gasps.

Thanh spoke rapidly with the commander. Alexander thought she said they should interrogate him at length later, but he was in too much pain for interpretation.

He was led out of the room, shoved down another tunnel, and thrown into a small, dark compartment. A guard bound his feet tightly at the ankles. The slightest movement forward or backward caused streaks of pain to flash through his chest and shoulders. He sat as motionless as possible, trying to distract his mind from the physical ache.

Why, he asked himself again, why do they want me? What will they do with me? Only his own will to live kept him from absolute despair, from believing that death could be more desirable than whatever was in store. Never before had he sensed his own mortality. The specter of death gripped his mind no less tightly than the ropes that bound his elbows and ankles. Bound, captured, lost in this maze of tunnels, he could not help but despair. Still, he would not give up hope, as he could not accept his own death. The fundamental instinct to survive became a primal link to all other living things, past, present and future. Reduced to the essence of living, teetering on the very edge of his own demise, he lapsed into semi-consciousness.

He was jerked alert by an ear-splitting explosion and a cataclysmic rush of wind. The walls surrounding him caved in, covering his legs with dirt and filling the air with dust and smoke. The deafening concussions continued, as if the bowels of the earth had erupted in a volcanic fury. What the shit? Then it dawned on him...B-52's! Sweet Jesus, they're bombing the bastards! Bomb the bastards, bury the bastards!

The explosions continued in rapid succession, cataclysmically unzipping the earth around him. Half-buried, his elation suddenly turned to fear. God damn, I'm being buried alive. Trapped by the bindings and the pain, he gasped for air, for a breath of oxygen. "God, dear God," he moaned.

He could hear cries from the tunnel, the sounds of people running and voices screaming in the dark. Footsteps stopped outside his cell and a flashlight shone in his face. He felt two quick jerks at his ropes, which made him cry out, and suddenly his arms fell forward, released. He was rolled over on his back and saw that it was Thanh, who was cutting the ropes on his ankles.

"Thanh," he said.

She did not look up until a third chop of her machete cut through the ropes. "Leave," she hissed. "Get out, now!" She looked at him for a brief second, then turned and fled back down the partially caved-in passageway.

Slowly he rose to his feet, bent over, numb, deaf, and bewildered. The narrow tunnel in front of him was pitch black. Not knowing where he was going, he cautiously stepped into the passageway, moving slowly forward, crawling through fallen sections of the tunnel complex. He came to the interrogation room where one lantern still provided a glimmer of light. The back wall had collapsed, and the table was buried.

He pressed on through the tunnel until he reached a wall of dirt. The loosely packed earth smelled of cordite. With the desperation of a terrified animal he clawed at the smoldering wall until it gave way. He fell forward, landing on his back in a bomb crater. Dazed and disoriented, the smoldering cordite stinging his lungs and choking him, he looked up and saw the faint silhouette of leaves above him. Slipping and falling backward, he began climbing until he finally reached the jagged edge of the crater.

It was dark and he could see nothing, but he could sense the forest around him. He inhaled, filling his lungs with fresh air, and crawled on hands and knees to a huge, fallen tree. Its limbs were shattered, and its trunk skewered toward the crater. Alexander grabbed the rough bark and stabilized himself. He shuffled onward until he found a path leading into the forest. The path opened into a large clearing where he recognized the remnants of a bunker which now lay crushed by the bombs. He had to find the stream and get to the Gulf and the junks.

Above the ringing in his ears he heard shouts, and dodged quickly behind a tree. Flashlight beams waved near the bamboo structures, and a group of Vietcong ran by. As soon as they passed, he scurried diagonally past another smoldering crater, and stepped into the jungle on the path that led toward the stream. He ran as fast as he could in the inky darkness. Freedom was all he could think about, and that meant the Gulf. Finally, after what seemed like an eternity, out of breath, and barely able to carry his own weight, he came to a clearing by the stream.

Were VC guarding the sampans? What if the boats were no longer there? Squirming into the jungle, he waited silently for several minutes, and then began creeping forward. He skirted the clearing until he reached the stream and promptly slid head first into the water. With only his face above the surface, he saw the sampans in front of him. He moved himself through the water to the first sampan and reached up for its bow line, quickly untied the knot, pulled the sampan parallel to the stream bank, and in one motion rolled into the empty vessel.

For nearly an hour he lay on his back motionless. The sluggish current carried the sampan downstream, further and further from the tunnel complex. He felt empty of will power, devoid of feeling or thought. Too much had happened too quickly. Time had at once collapsed and been suspended. Only twenty-four hours ago he and the Dai Uy were

214

hiding across from the VC collection point, and less than twelve hours ago they had not entered the village. How could so much change so quickly, so irrevocably?

It took a great deal of effort to raise himself upright. He found the starter cord, took it in both hands, and threw himself backwards. He felt a sense of rejuvenation and, at the same time, apprehension as the motor sputtered to life. Instinctively he decided that speed rather than stealth was his best ally. He opened the throttle and ripped down the winding waterway, oblivious to the overhanging limbs and sharp turns. Several times he sideswiped the muddy bank, but freedom felt as tangible now as the tree limbs that slapped his face.

Gradually the light of dawn penetrated the thick foliage, making his progress easier. He kept the throttle wide open as he weaved toward the Gulf. The stream emptied into the canal by the village, which he saw had been flattened and burnt. The American choppers had evidently hit the village after he had been captured. He saw no signs of life. Without looking back at the village, he sped down the wide canal to the coast. When his sampan entered the waters of the Gulf he plowed into the rolling surf. He inhaled the salty sea breeze and felt an overwhelming sense of sheer elation. He was free.

Less than a quarter mile away he saw two junks. He stood up in the sampan, waving and yelling as loud as he could. From his level near the Gulf's surface his eyes were drawn to the painting on their bows, to the eyes of the dragon. Were they symbols of good luck or of evil? He pulled alongside the junk where Sanchez stood. Several hands reached out to help him. He winced when they tugged him to the deck. The Vietnamese sailors were jabbering, trying to shake his hand or pat his back. Sanchez ordered everyone to move back, then put his arm around Alexander for support.

"You don't look so hot."

Alexander sobbed. "Oh, shit, Sanchez," was all he could say. "It's good to see you."

Sanchez reached down, lifted him up, and carried him to the Dai Uy's cabin and carefully lay him in the hammock. Except for a dislocated jaw and tender feet, Alexander was physically unharmed. Yet emotionally, spiritually, and psychologically he had crossed a bridge that could never be retraced.

Sanchez ordered a cup of tea for Alexander and then briefed him on their response to the ambush. He had received Alexander's radio message, scrambled the Seawolves, loaded the sampans with sailors, and made his way up the canal to the village. By the time the choppers arrived night had completely fallen. With the choppers overhead for support, Sanchez and the sailors entered the village, met no resistance, and found seven dead sailors shot in the head and two dead Vietcong. They had carried the bodies to a junk which had returned to Rach Gia. The villagers had either escaped or left with the VC, so after looking for Alexander, Sanchez had directed the choppers to flatten the village. Alexander was the only one of the group unaccounted for.

"We looked for you last night, but it was too dark to do any good. I knew you weren't in the village. I figured you'd been wounded and crawled for cover. I wasn't going to report you missing until we knew for sure. We were just preparing to search for you. What happened?"

Alexander related the story of his capture and escape, which sounded unbelievable. If his feet, shoulders, and jaw weren't so sore he might doubt it himself. In Vietnam time stood still or raced forward, in either case creating a sense of unreality.

"The Dai Uy never knew what hit him," Alexander said quietly. "He was twenty feet from me. Alive one second," he snapped his fingers, "and dead the next." Alexander placed a hand over his eyes as though trying to blot out the image of the Dai Uy crumpling to the ground. He finished the tea and lay back in the hammock, completely washed out.

Sanchez put Alexander aboard the other junk and sent him back to Hon Tre. On the trip to the island Alexander fell into a deep sleep. When he awoke he saw the familiar bay with the coconut palms swaying peacefully on the beach. Nothing had changed on the island.

# Chapter XX

A new Vietnamese lieutenant was brought in from An Thoi to replace the Dai Uy. Lieutenant Trung was more formal and reserved than the Dai Uy. He was accompanied by two junior grade lieutenants, bringing to six the number of Vietnamese officers in the coastal group. After his first meeting with Lt. Trung, Alexander realized that Vietnamese/American relations had permanently changed. Rapport, he realized, was really a matter of personal accord.

The U Minh campaign was deemed a success by both the Americans and the Vietnamese. Westmoreland's war of attrition had been replaced by General Creighton Abrams' strategy of cordon-and-pile-on, to surround the expected enemy stronghold and then use the awesome firepower of B-52's to hammer the enemy into defeat or disarray. Combined with pacification of the countryside, the strategy was aimed at allowing Nixon's Vietnamization program time to succeed. More and more combat operations were being turned over to the Vietnamese. American forces in Vietnam had shrunk from 519,000 at its peak to 184,000. America was going home.

Three weeks after the U Minh operation, Alexander was still emotionally drained. He could only sleep for short periods and had no appetite. He kept mainly to the hootch, reading or talking to Oink. He had written a lengthy report to An Thoi about the firefight at Ap Lon village, describing as best he could where the tunnel complex was located, and the possible sapper attack on Nam Can.

Even Owens' exuberance over the new chicken coop failed to perk him up. With only six weeks left on his tour of duty, he self-diagnosed his malaise as short-timer's fever and methodically crossed out each day on his calendar.

*March 1, 1971*
*Dear Alex:*

*Another first of the month! God, I do love them so. I count my time from the firsts of months now, under the assumption that I can spend the last fifteen days standing on my head in cat shit and still be ecstatic. Think of it: only six weeks to go. Argghh.*

*I heard about your ambush. Sorry about the Dai Uy. He was the best of the lot, but just be thankful you're safe.*

*I just got a Dear John letter from Brenda. "Our relationship is over" because I don't love her. I guess I tried too hard. The ironic thing is that I was at last beginning to appreciate her for more than a good sport and a passionate piece of ass. But we will "always be good friends". You know how valuable that is. If we had ever been good friends, it might be possible, but we were good lovers from the start and nothing less. Guess her Puritan values finally caught up with her, or more likely, someone else is sharing her sack. She's been too busy to write more than two letters in the last month, and it's suddenly not good enough to meet in Hawaii after I leave this hole. If she has another lover, I just hope to hell she doesn't let him use my car.*

*Her timing was brilliant. She waited until I already had my DEROS application in before deciding to accept what she's known all along. You know what a joy Hawaii is for a single man — a monastery with real live hallucinations. So I'm cancelling that trip.*

*To celebrate my new-found freedom, I have a proposal for you. After DEROS, when our sentence is over, let's take the circuitous way back to the States. We can go by embassy flight through India, the mid-East, and Europe. Neither of us will ever be twenty-five, single, or independent again. What do you think, buddy?*

*Let's get together in Saigon on the fifteenth and talk this over. I'm going nuts here. I need to get out of Vietnam and taste the wine of civilization. And soon, very soon.*

*Did you know VN pigs shit white because of all the rice in their diet? I discovered that while watching a huge boar foul the decks of my junk last trip from An Thoi. By the way, what color is yours getting to be?*

*Shalom, Dave*

Alexander smiled and put down Holloman's letter. His concentration for several days had been distracted by continuous thoughts of Thanh. Holloman's letter gave him the impetus to act. He stood and strapped on his .38, picked up his binoculars, and walked out the advisor's hootch, yelling at Oink to stay put. Kicking aside coconut shells and pig shit, he strode through the village to Sanchez' and Tho's house.

"Hello," said Sanchez, yawning. At midday only the insects stirred. "What's going on?"

"I wanted you to know I'm going up the mountain. If I'm not back until tomorrow morning, don't worry."

"Why are you going there?"

"I met an old Buddhist up there. I want to talk to him. Don't worry. I just wanted you to know where I was. How's Tho feeling?"

"Fine. She's beginning to look pregnant."

"I'll be in Saigon next week with Lieutenant Holloman and will run the traps for your marriage papers again. See you tomorrow."

Alexander returned to the village and followed the path leading up the mountain. He began the ascent, climbing through tall coconut palms, past the huge granite boulders, through thick patches of tamarind trees and scattered banana plots. Steadily and methodically he gained altitude. From time to time he paused to catch his breath. At this altitude the air was clear and cooler than in the village. Salty perspiration stung the heat rash in his crotch and under his arms. Occasionally he caught glimpses of the thatched roofs of the village below, which from his perspective looked like tiny, rectangular chips spread along a thin silver line of beach.

The small house on the far side of the banana trees stood exactly as he remembered. He carefully examined the area for signs of activity. Seeing nothing unusual, he un-holstered his gun and cautiously stepped through the banana fronds to the flimsy door. He tapped on its base with his foot and heard a shuffle of feet inside. The door opened, revealing the expressionless face of the old monk. Without speaking, the monk turned and walked back into the hut, leaving the door ajar. Alexander followed him inside. The old monk moved to the far side of the room where he sat down on a straw mat, crossed his feet, and closed his eyes.

After becoming accustomed to the dark interior, Alexander sat down at the table and put the binoculars to his eyes. He peered through them for a long time, meticulously scanning the Gulf and the distant mainland. He found his junks anchored offshore the Three Sisters. Hundreds of fishing boats bobbed in the dun and ginger-colored water. Finally he put down the binoculars and walked outside the house. He searched the area nearby but did not find what he sought and returned to the house.

"Has anyone come here before with binoculars?" Alexander spoke in Vietnamese, slowly and deliberately.

The Buddhist opened his eyes and gazed at Alexander. Deliberately he rose to his feet, walked over to a small kerosene burner, and put on a pan of water to heat. After a few moments, he shuffled to the table, carefully poured tea into two cups, and sat down opposite Alexander.

"Why do you come here? What do you seek?" the old man asked.

"Have men come here before with binoculars?" repeated Alexander.

Alexander could only understand part of the Buddhist's response, but the gist of it was how much he abhorred the war.

"So many dead," Alexander concurred softly.

The Buddhist closed his eyes and said nothing. Alexander's eyes swept the panorama. From this vantage, the Gulf between Hon Tre and Rach Gia could be easily monitored, and the junks positions could be relayed by radio or mirrors to the Three Sisters.

"Your niece, Thanh, believes in the war."

Again the bonze opened his eyes.

"She saved my life. I would like to thank her."

"She is no longer here," replied the old Buddhist. "She is in France. What are you searching for?"

Alexander stared out the open window, not certain of the answer. The scene looked like a Chinese painting. Several minutes passed in silence. "Do others come to your house to observe the Gulf?"

"It is peaceful here. I would like peace to return to my country."

Alexander looked at the old man and nodded.

The Buddhist looked deep into Alexander's eyes.

"Perhaps one day you will find peace," he said and wearily shuffled back to the dark interior away from the window, sat down on a straw mat and again shut his eyes.

Alexander was not sure what to do. He had expected to uncover a VC observation post and was not certain he had not done so. He wondered if his host, like so many in this country, concealed a pervasive duplicity. Nothing in this country, he thought, is as it appears on the surface.

Alexander stared at the monk sitting cross-legged on the mat with eyes closed and face devoid of expression. He moved next to the old Buddhist, sat down, crossed his legs, and closed his own eyes.

At first his mind flitted in different directions. He thought of the last year, of Thanh, of the Dai Uy and the ambush. Gradually, like the movement of a shadow, he became aware of the sounds around him. He heard the crackling of the thatch in the wind. The breeze seemed to speak to him. His knees became numb and his legs began to ach. He recalled the night in the U Minh before the VC arrived, and tried to rekindle that comprehension of the present.

Dusk slowly discharged the light in the small hut, altering the wall's hue from dull yellow to soft magenta. Finally only the kerosene lantern on the table glowed warm and bright, like a genie alive and playful in its glass cage. Alexander's consciousness of his discomfort seemed to peel away. He recalled Wordsworth's "Intimation of Immortality" and his mind began to drift like a boat on the sea.

It was dawn when Alexander again became conscious of his surroundings. A fresh, savory smell of cooking rice filled the hut. Opening his eyes, he saw the monk standing over the stove. Alexander unfolded his legs, which felt as if they had been perforated with a thousand tiny pins. He rose and nearly fell backward. With effort he reached the table, sat down, and lifted the small round porcelain bowl to his lip. The taste was like an extract of the natural grain. He chewed slowly, absorbing each mouthful of rice into the pores of his taste buds. When he finished he handed the old Buddhist his bowl.

"Thank you."

The sound of his own words pierced the silence like a gunshot and brought Alexander's mind back to his business. Goddamn it, he mumbled to himself. He put the binoculars to his eyes, again scanned the Gulf, and then placed the binocular straps over his head, picked up his .38, and walked to the door.

The hollowed eyes of the old Buddhist watched him.

"Do not be suspicious of the true dragon."

Alexander had no idea what the monk meant, but he nodded. It was a phrase that would haunt him for years. Inhaling deeply, he stepped out of the door and began his journey down the mountain.

# Chapter XXI

Holloman was already at the terrace bar. Several empty glasses were on his table. He was wearing civilian clothing and a black bandana tied around his forehead. When he saw Alexander, he smiled and flashed his friend the peace symbol.

"Hey, *amigo,* you look like a scriptwriter for the underground press," quipped Alexander.

"It's more my style. The military crap-o is poisoning my mind. Say, you're looking good. Wearing a hat, I see. I read the report on your shoot 'em-up. I'm truly sorry about the Dai Uy, Alex. He was the best."

They ordered drinks and leaned back in their chairs. The mid-morning traffic had not yet reached its afternoon frenzy. A shoeshine boy lazily pointed to their boots, then ambled to the next table.

"Less than a month to DEROS, Holloman, can you believe it? In one way it seems like we've been here ten years, and sometimes it seems like ten minutes."

"You may have a month, Lieutenant, but I already got my ticket on the Freedom Bird," responded Holloman, holding up an index finger wrapped in gauze and adhesive tape.

"What are you talking about? The only early out for you will be in a body bag. Got your ticket, *bullshitiando*."

"Look here, buddy, look at this little jewel." Holloman began removing the bandage. "Here, you see that?" Holloman waved his index finger in front of Alexander's face. Where there should have been skin and muscle next to the fingernail was a large cavity. The smell was awful.

"What is it?" asked Alexander, moving his head away from the rotting finger.

"That's all there is. A black hole. Some unidentified oriental bacteria is eating me alive. The med's can't figure it out so, I'm going stateside tomorrow at 0900. Already got my orders."

Alexander looked again at the finger Holloman held in front of him. "You're shitting me, Holloman. Well, that beats all. No telling where that finger's been. I'm surprised it isn't your middle finger. And now they're discharging you because of a social disease?"

"Yep. An unidentified finger organism, a UFO, and here I come, USA. Which leaves us with less than twenty-four hours to celebrate. So down the hatch."

Holloman turned up his drink and ordered everyone at the bar a round. The thought of leaving

Nam, more than of returning home, had lifted his spirits. After a few more drinks, they caught a cyclo to the Vietnamese Air Force O-Club at Ton Son Nhut. When they entered the back bar, their two girls recognized them and gave them welcoming hugs. By late afternoon both Americans were three sheets to the wind. Any anxiety about the Vietnamese flyboys was long dispelled. In the dark bar they pulled off the girls' *ao dais* and made love on the soft leather seats of the high-backed booths, joking with each other under the table top. By the time a crowd of fighter pilots arrived, Holloman told Alexander he was ready to leave.

"Leave? No way, Holloman," said Alexander. "I like this place. It's beginning to feel like home."

"Wait till you see the next delight. Come on, Alex, it's not far."

The two argued, but this time Holloman prevailed. Reluctantly Alexander told the girls they had to leave, and tipped them generously. As they walked out the main gate, Holloman saluted the gate guard, and said to his friend, "Alex, did you hear about the gang of teenage gooks who tried to castrate an American soldier right here a couple of months ago?"

"Now you tell me. No doubt it was for screwing their women. Come on, let's go back to the O-Club."

"No, no, no." said Holloman, grabbing his arm. "Just want you to keep your guard up. This is the Nam, buddy. Hey!" He stopped a cyclo and gave the driver directions.

The cyclo driver took them down Le Loc Boulevard, turned on a side street, and stopped at the entrance to a narrow an alley. Holloman stepped out, paid the driver, and proceeded to enter the dark alleyway.

"Where you going? Jesus Christ, Holloman, this ain't no place for gringos."

"Faith, my son, just keep the faith and follow me."

Holloman disappeared around a corner and Alexander hesitantly trailed after him. The alley wound through a barrio of tin houses made of cardboard and crushed beer cans. Large concrete sewage pipes used as living quarters also lined the alleyway. When the two passed open doorways, old Vietnamese men and *mama-sans* stared at the two Americans. Children yelled at them and grabbed their hands for souvenirs. The alleyway smelled of raw sewage mixed with *nuoc mam* and cooking oils. Holloman walked through the maze without hesitation, stopped at a nondescript domicile, and knocked on the door. A small sliding window opened, and then the door opened.

"Where have you taken me? What kind of goddamn place is this?" asked Alexander.

"Welcome to Mom's Magic Shop. Come on."

After entering and walking down a dark hallway, they were greeted by a fat middle-age *mama-san* draped in gaudy jewelry.

"Meet the lady of the house," Holloman said.

"Hello, *mama-san. Toi kong biet tieng Viet.*" She nodded and smiled, revealing betel-stained gums.

"Follow me," said Holloman.

They passed a doorway and entered a dimly lit room. Several elaborately-carved wooden bunks lined up along one wall. Velvet curtains hung in front of most of them, providing a modicum of privacy. American rock music played softly in the background.

"Holloman, I've seen better flop houses in Ojinaga, Mexico. I ain't discriminating, but we can do better than this. No telling what the women look like. That oriental bacteria is eating your brain."

"No, no, no. Come on, I'll show you." Holloman walked over to a Vietnamese man, whispered for a few seconds, then handed him some money. "Come on."

Holloman led Alexander to one of the bunks. The Vietnamese man came back with a two-foot long, curved smoking pipe, and handed it to Holloman.

"What the shit?" asked Alexander.

"Opium, man, nirvana in a noodle. Here, try it."

Holloman lit the pipe and handed it to Alexander. He took the pipe and hesitantly inhaled a draw. The smoke was pungent yet sweet. He exhaled and returned the pipe to Holloman. "Shit, David, this is too much. Let's go on back to Tu Do."

"No, no, no. Try it. Just try one pipe. This is the ultimate reality. It makes it all worthwhile," Holloman said and fell back on the bunk, grasping the pipe.

Alexander stared at his friend for a few seconds. Holloman was already lost to the pipe. Alexander knelt down, took the pipe, and pulled Holloman up by the shoulders.

"Holloman, I'm leaving. This isn't for me. Listen, you be careful, you hear? Don't forget your flight tomorrow. Holloman." He pulled Holloman's head to his chest and hugged him. "Keep it in the road, *amigo*. Let me hear from you."

"Sure, sure, buddy," said Holloman. "It's a hell of a war, huh?" With his bandaged hand he flashed Alexander the peace symbol. Alexander let him go and he fell back on the bunk, clinging to the pipe.

Alexander stood up and walked out. "The Age of Aquarius" pulsated softly in the background.

# Chapter XXII

The next morning Alexander awoke with a splitting headache and a bitter taste in his mouth. He wondered whether Holloman had caught his flight. After breakfast he checked again on the status of Sanchez' marriage application, which the clerk promised would be processed by the end of the month.

In the afternoon Alexander bought a Graham Greene book and was reading it at the Continental terrace bar. The book had been written in the very place he was sitting. Tomorrow he intended to return to Hon Tre. For now, he wanted only to sit alone and read.

The area in front of the National Assembly had been blocked off by the police in anticipation of an anti-government rally later in the day. The adjacent street bustled with cyclo, car, and bicycle traffic, and the sidewalks were filled with pedestrians bustling to their various pursuits.

"Thought I'd find you here."

Alexander glanced up. The Colonel was standing at his table. Alexander rose to greet the Colonel. Since he was not wearing a hat, he did not salute but instead offered his hand. "Colonel, sir, what brings you to Saigon? This is a surprise."

"I'm attending briefings at MACV. Commander Schoen said I'd find you here."

Alexander didn't know Schoen knew anything about his Saigon escapades with Holloman, but then they had not kept them a secret.

"Have a seat, Colonel. Could I buy you a drink?" offered Alexander.

"Don't mind if I do. Is this place secure?" the Colonel asked, glancing at the outdoor bar with its archways that opened to the streets.

Although the Continental wasn't far from the Brinks Hotel where several Americans had been killed early in the war, Alexander assured him it was as safe as any other place in a city that experienced terrorist attacks.

"I was sorry to hear about your counterpart," said the Colonel. "He seemed like an aggressive type, the kind of leader this country needs. That's the one weak link in this Vietnamization program — effective leadership. Too goddamn many politicians are calling the shots."

After the waiter dropped off their drinks, Alexander asked a question that had been troubling him. "Colonel, do you consider the U Minh operation a success?" He had asked himself the question many times. Was it really worth it?

"Hell yes, it was a success. Our operations in the U Minh are mop-ups. We're tightening the cordon. Ever since the Cambodian incursion, the VC have been kicked out of the Delta. We've effectively won the war."

Alexander was surprised at such optimism. The Colonel had served three previous tours in Vietnam and understood its politics. Although he was never in doubt, his perspective of the war was well-founded. The rest of the afternoon they discussed the effectiveness of the Vietnamese army and navy, the American troop withdrawal, and various other topics related to the American military presence.

When dusk fell Alexander suggested they go to one of his favorite Vietnamese restaurant. The Colonel told him he didn't use chopsticks, hated rice, and couldn't stand the stench of *nuoc mam*, but Alexander convinced him, anyway. They took a taxi to a rooftop restaurant overlooking the Saigon River. The place was crowded with well-dressed Vietnamese and a scattering of Americans. An orchestra played Vietnamese music, its atonal chords blending perfectly with the clear voice of a beautiful, young vocalist who sang ballads lamenting the war.

Alexander ordered a six-course meal of fresh fish, squid, scallops, and crab. For the Colonel he ordered beef cooked in seven different styles. When the Colonel tasted the first dish, Alexander smiled at his reaction.

"Lieutenant, this is delicious. I didn't know Vietnamese food could taste so good. It makes me think the old French colonists lived the high life, don't you think?"

"They probably did," replied Alexander, "but then colonialism is long dead."

"Right. Maybe I was born too damn late," mused the Colonel. "Still, this isn't a bad time or a bad place. It's sure as hell the perfect war."

"What do you mean, the perfect war?" asked Alexander.

"War gives military men a sense of achievement," the Colonel responded. "It doesn't have to be a big war, just a nice little war in a third-world country where the food is good and the climate is acceptable. Vietnam gets a little hot and muggy, but it's nothing like Washington DC in August. Yes sir, it's the perfect war. Here we've got complete mobility, absolute control of the air, and a superiority of firepower that has never been so mismatched in the history of warfare. Lieutenant, for a military man, it just doesn't get any better."

"I never thought of it quite like that, Colonel."

"Don't be naive, Lieutenant. There have always been wars, and always will be. Show me one six-month period in human history when there wasn't a war. Peaceniks are nothing but damn fools, and piss poor historians to boot. And if we're going to be in a war, which no world power can avoid, then this is the best kind."

Alexander shook his head at the novelty of the thought. "And what about all the dead and wounded and their families? Are they better off with war or without war?"

"I'm not talking about human misery. I'm talking about human nature. War is a fundamental element of human existence. And if you put it in perspective, this one isn't bad, not bad at all. Here, let's drink to that." The Colonel clanked his glass against Alexander's.

"You said we have already won the war. Do you believe it?"

"Knocking out the Cambodian sanctuaries last year assured its success."

"And do you think the Vietnamese can pick up the ball? It's obvious we're leaving."

"They need better leadership. And we'll need to provide air support for a few more years to keep Hanoi from concentrating their forces for a conventional invasion. We've won the war, but can still lose the peace."

"Yes," agreed Alexander, "except there is the one ingredient you're overlooking, sir."

"What's that?" asked the Colonel.

"The tenacity of the Vietcong. In a contest between firepower and will power, which would win? A year ago I'd have picked firepower. Now I'm not so sure."

"Firepower can win, if we have the will power to use it."

"That's a big 'if,' Colonel. Ten years from now we'll know the answer. The perfect war...you've got to be kidding."

# Chapter XXIII

Back at Hon Tre Alexander occupied himself with the details of daily living. The new base commander remained in camp coordinating logistics, and sent his staff officers on patrol. Alexander met with him, by appointment only, in a small office at the operations hut. He wanted Alexander to requisition more materials from the Americans, particularly sodium carbide lamps for the base perimeter even though the generators would only run sixty-watt bulbs.

Owens' chicken and pig operation was proving a success. Already several of the village sows were sucking litters of pink and black piglets, and more than a thousand chicks were being fed oven-dried fish remains bought from the villagers.

One afternoon after the water taxi brought ice to the local bar, Owens and Alexander walked to the local bar for a beer. When Owens expressed enthusiasm for the chicken business, Alexander remained quiet.

"Captain," said Owens to Alexander, "you ain't been yourself lately. I seen you acting like some kind of Buddhist monk, sitting cross-legged with your eyes closed. Reminds me of a preacher with a guilty conscience. Now what's the matter with you?"

"Nothing, Owens, except that I'm getting short."

"That's what I need to talk to you about, sir. Now listen, captain, about your investment here."

"I'm glad you brought that up. I've been thinking about how to transfer title," said Alexander.

"Transfer title? We're in this boat together. Hold your horses, Geronimo. What you need to do is open your eyes and let the sun shine in."

"And what does that mean?" asked Alexander.

"Just look there," Owens said, pointing to the chicken coop. "You are looking at a gold mine. You know how much it cost to raise them eleven hundred fryers?"

Alexander shook his head.

"It cost one hundred-and-ninety-eight dollars total, and that includes fish guts, feathers, and fuel for the generator. Less than two hundred bucks, and it'll soon convert to five thousand dollars. Shee-it, man, we're chicken billionaires." He began snapping his fingers. "There's one thing, though." Owens added. "You got to re-up."

"No way, Owens...another year of crotch rot, and my legs will fall off. I've been thinking about it, and here's what I'll do," said Alexander. "I'll get all my loan back from the first sale of chickens. My and the Dai Uy's share of any profits are to be allocated for village improvements."

Alexander believed as much as Owens that the chicken operation would be a financial success, but his mind was made up. "Owens, if you ever get off this island, look me up, and maybe we'll start us a pig and chicken operation in the States. But not here. I'm going home."

Ten days before DEROS, Sanchez accompanied Alexander on his final Market Time patrol. The two Americans threw their gear on the old Kien Giang class junk, which pitched like a pump jack, but was nevertheless their favorite junk. Its bow turned up jauntily, and its cabin, perched on the stern like an afterthought, gave it the appearance of a miniature three-masted ship of the line, centuries out of place.

The breeze held steady and cool. Huge thunderheads built up in the afternoons, anticipating the coming monsoons. The moon rose like an orange jackfruit above the horizon. The vastness of the dun-colored Gulf and the expanse of blue-black sky were exhilarating to Alexander. Rising early, he and Sanchez witnessed the drama of sunrise at sea. When the grey semi-light of dawn changed to mauve, reducing the stately moon to a pale orb, the golden yellow sunrays touched the upper reaches of the thunderheads and imperceptibly moved down their faces in an ageless salutation. By midday the sky was blunt, reflecting a thousand moving mirrors on the choppy surface. Gradually the sun set, once again painting the towering clouds gold and pink and magenta, as if conducted by a symphonic maestro sans sound.

They toured the entire Nine Foxtrot area, first going north to the necklace of small islands which Alexander and the Dai Uy had visited shortly before moving the coastal group to Hon Tre. Nothing had changed in the small fishing villages. Life continued to be dictated by the rhythms of the sea and the weather. The junks then went to Hon Re in the deep waters on the western edge of the patrol area. In another place or time the blue-green ocean and sparkling white beaches would be swarming with tourists. Back on the shallow coastal shelf of the mainland, hundreds of small fishing boats combed the brown waters, harvesting an abundance of sea life in a centuries old activity. The junks perfunctorily checked the fishermen's identification papers, often accepting a few fish or vegetables.

After supper Alexander and Sanchez and several of the sailors played gin rummy by the light of kerosene lanterns. A year earlier everything about the Vietnamese — their food, music, conversation, and behavior — had seemed so foreign to Alexander. Now he felt at home in their world.

"Sanchez, are you going to re-up?" asked Alexander casually. "Where will you and Tho raise your kids?"

"Our marriage papers should be finalized soon. I think it's time for a tour stateside."

"And what does Tho think?"

"She's ready to go, too. Her family doesn't accept our marriage."

"You think she'll like the States?" asked Alexander.

"There's only one way to find out," replied Sanchez. "What are you going to do when you get back?"

"As Holloman would say, dog ass me, cow shit I know," smiled Alexander as he gazed up at the twinkling stars. "I think I'll go back the long way, maybe stopover in France. In two months I'll be out of the Navy. Maybe I'll go to Alaska and give this goddamn heat rash a good dose of cold weather. One thing is certain. The winds are changing, like the coming monsoons."

The third evening the boats rounded the eastern tip of Hon Tre, rolled into the bay, and dropped anchor. Alexander looked thoughtfully at the new lights on the base perimeter and at the large chicken coop, tangible signs of a contribution that he was proud of.

A sampan pulled up to their junk to take Alexander, Sanchez, and the young Vietnamese ensign ashore. After they loaded their gear and stepped aboard, a Vietnamese sailor carrying a large duffle jumped from the junk's deck onto the sampan's gunwale. In the flash of an eye the sampan tipped. Alexander and Sanchez came up sputtering and cursing. The young ensign swam to the anchor rope and started shouting, angry at this loss of face. The rest of the crew and everyone on the beach thought the incident was hilarious.

Alexander ordered one of the sailors still on the junk to retrieve his and Sanchez's gear and take it to the advisors' hootch. The two Americans then swam to shore where Brooks and Owens greeted them with broad smiles.

"Hey, captain," said Owens, slapping his thighs and laughing, "you look like MacArthur reclaiming the Philippines. Too bad we ain't got the newsreels."

"Hello, men," said Alexander in mock seriousness as he stepped, dripping wet, onto the beach. "On this, the occasion of my last Coastal Group 43 patrol and my first amphib landing, I feel it is my solemn duty to...buy the drinks. Let's hit the bar."

He led the group along the beach where they sat at a table under the coconut palms and drank lukewarm beer until well past midnight. Owens had sold the first bunch of fryers at the Rach Gia Market. He handed Alexander a huge wad of piasters.

"What am I supposed to do with this?" asked Alexander.

"Shit man, that's your slice. Ain't it sweet, bo-peep? Forty-eight thousand piasters. We gonna be rich, even at the black market rate."

"I just thought of something," said Alexander laughing.

"What's that, Captain? You change your mind about leaving this honey bucket?" asked Owens.

"Nope. But I don't have time to convert all this play money to dollars. The gendarmes would think I've been dealing in dope. Guess I have a week to blow it. Come on men, let's call it a day."

The group disbursed, Sanchez heading up the path to his thatched house, Owens to the quarters he had constructed at the coop, and Brooks and Alexander back to the hootch.

Chapter XXIV

Alexander's replacement arrived less than a week before DEROS. Lieutenant Richards was fifty pounds overweight and was obviously unhappy with his assignment in the boondocks. Alexander introduced him to the other advisors and to the base commander, and gave him a thumbnail sketch of what to expect. Mainly, he recommended, lean on Sanchez's expertise and judgment until he had his feet on the ground. The new lieutenant refused to touch the Vietnamese food served by the one-eyed cook.

On Alexander's last night at Hon Tre, several of the young Vietnamese officers came to the advisors' hootch to wish him goodbye. They stayed for several hours, drinking *ba-xi-day*, and chattering about the past year. Alexander let Oink join the party. The animal, which now weighed nearly three hundred pounds, slurped pans of warm beer with audible pleasure. Late in the night the Vietnamese staggered out the door, each giving Alexander a hug as he left.

Richards had long ago fallen asleep on Alexander's bunk and was snoring worse than Oink, who was asleep under the hammock. Alexander walked out the compound gate and up to the thatched house, where Sanchez and Tho gave him a mattress and pillow for the night.

The next day the new commander assigned the Kien Giang junk to take Alexander to Rach Gia at noon. There he could catch a chopper to An Thoi for out-processing. In the morning Alexander packed his belongings into a duffle bag and assigned the KAK codes and Starlight scope to Lt. Richards. He gave Flop and Bitch a good back scratch and then sat down on the steps and talked to Oink, rubbing the base of the pig's ears. He rose, wished Richards good luck, and left the hootch without looking back. When he rounded the corner of the operations hut, he stopped short. Standing at attention in rows were all the Vietnamese sailors, dressed in their best U.S. Navy-issue blues. In front of them were the Vietnamese officers, the commander, Sanchez, Owens, and Brooks.

Alexander gazed at the sailors. By American standards it was a ragtag parade. Maybe half of them wore hats and fewer wore shoes. Their shirts were faded and wrinkled. He walked up to the commander and saluted. The commander, with severe formality, returned the salute, read a lengthy commendation, and pinned a South Vietnamese medal to Alexander's lapel. After receiving the medal Alexander requested that he speak to the sailors. The commander nodded his assent.

"Today I leave Hon Tre to return to my country. Like myself, most of the American soldiers in Vietnam will soon return to America. We did not come to fight your war for you. South Vietnam is your country. It is up to you, not America, to keep South Vietnam a strong nation. I wish you good luck. I will think of you often."

Alexander strode to the three American advisors and shook their hands. Sanchez snapped to a smart salute, the first he had given Alexander, and the other advisors and the entire coastal group followed suit. Alexander returned the salutes. Too choked for words, he turned and walked out the gate.

A number of villagers had gathered along the beach. As he stepped through the crowd he saw Tho, now looking very pregnant, and silently nodded goodbye to her. A sailor loaded his duffle into a sampan and paddled him to the waiting junk. The sailors onboard shouted and threw colored smoke grenades, and someone shot several M-16 clips into the air. The junk weighed anchor and pointed toward the mainland. Alexander watched the figures on the beach until they receded into tiny dots.

At Rach Gia Alexander stopped by the old dilapidated Navy building to out-process with the NILOS. After the brief turnover procedure one of the NILOS offered to have his driver take Alexander to the airport.

When they reached the central market Alexander directed the driver to turn down a side street. The driver maneuvered into the smaller street and followed directions until Alexander indicated to stop next to a green iron gate. Alexander hesitated for a moment, then stepped to the gate and knocked loudly. No one answered. He walked back to the jeep and told the driver to proceed to the airport.

"Who lives there, sir?" asked the young corporal. "You got a Vietnamese girlfriend?"

"Not exactly," Alexander replied. "Just an old acquaintance. How long you been in Nam?"

"Four months," answered the driver. "Seems like four years."

Within an hour Alexander caught a chopper headed to An Thoi. As it ascended above the landscape he once again observed the country's pastoral charm and spurious simplicity.

At An Thoi he reported to Commander Shoen, who lauded his efforts over the past year. That evening Alexander paid the bar at the officer's club. He hardly recognized a face. All his friends had already rotated back to the States.

The next day he hitched a ride to the airstrip for a flight to Saigon. No one saw him off. He left IV Corp headquarters, and three days later South Vietnam, the same way he had arrived a year ago: unannounced, and outwardly as unchanged as the peaceful countryside below him.

## THE END

In the final analysis, it is their war. They are the ones who have to win it or lose it. We can help them, but they have to win it, the people of Vietnam.

John F. Kennedy
September 2, 1963

In the end, the attempt to "build a nation" did fail. The effort to protect the villages often did lead to their destruction. And the struggle to win the hearts and minds of Vietnamese peasants did seem to engender more hostility than friendship. But this was neither the result of evil intentions nor a wanton disregard for human life. The truth was far more complex, and far more tragic.

*A Collision of Cultures, The Vietnam Experience*
The Boston Publishing Company, 1984

# ABOUT THE AUTHOR

Sam L. Pfiester served two tours in Vietnam, the second as a senior advisor to a Vietnamese river patrol group along the Cambodian border. He was awarded the Bronze Star and the Vietnam Service Medal, First Class. *The Perfect War* is based on his experiences. He has also written *The Golden Lane: Faja de Oro* about the Tampico Oil Boom 1909-1914. He and his wife have three children and live in Georgetown, Texas.

13964346R00136

Made in the USA
Charleston, SC
11 August 2012